Hallmark
PUBLISHING

A CHRISTMAS TO
REMEMBER

Based on the Hallmark Channel Original Movie

REBECCA MOESTA

A Christmas to Remember
Copyright @ 2018 Crown Media Family Networks

Print ISBN: 978-1-947892-23-1
Ebook ISBN: 978-1-947892-22-4

Hallmark
PUBLISHING

www.hallmarkpublishing.com
For more about the movie visit:
www.hallmarkchannel.com/a-christmas-to-remember

TABLE OF CONTENTS

CHAPTER 1

Christmas was a magical time of year in New York. Wollman Rink was open in Central Park, and a gigantic Christmas tree graced Rockefeller Plaza. Holiday music was ubiquitous, and strains of songs like "All I Want for Christmas," "It's the Most Wonderful Time of the Year," and "Sleigh Ride" seemed to follow Jennifer Wade everywhere she went.

Lights twinkled on buildings, trees, and food carts. A faint dusting of snow still clung to the grass in the parks that Jennifer passed as she walked at a brisk pace from the subway to the Kitchen Network building where she worked. Wreaths hung from lampposts. The smells of hot cocoa with cinnamon and roasting nuts made her mouth water. There was no time to enjoy the Christmassy sights and sounds, though.

She had a TV show to record, and she didn't want to be late. After all, the popular weekly show *Homestyle with Jennifer Wade* on the Kitchen Network was named for her. Posters for *Homestyle* were plastered all over New York City—even on the sides of busses.

Being on billboards and busses came with a certain level of pressure. She didn't take the responsibility lightly and made sure that each show was polished down to the last detail. That's what her viewers had come to expect of her, and she demanded no less of herself.

This morning they were taping Jennifer's Christmas special, and she wanted everything to be perfect. But nothing ever was, was it? There was always some aspect that could be improved. Had she forgotten anything? She couldn't shake a faint feeling of worry that hovered at the edge of her thoughts, spurring her to walk faster.

Once inside the network building, she rushed through hair and makeup, then changed into the outfit she had chosen after spending almost two days trying on various possibilities. Elegant, yet simple, it complemented her dyed-blonde hair and pale skin.

"Oh, my gosh, I hope we got this wardrobe looking right," Jennifer said to the wardrobe assistant, Aimee, as they headed through the soundstage toward the set. Dressed in a sweatshirt and jeans, with her hair up in a ponytail, the girl seemed young, and Jennifer tried to impress on her how important clothing choices were. Of course, the crew of the show didn't always appreciate her penchant for perfectionism. Around the set, they joked that there were two ways of doing anything: Jennifer's way and the wrong way.

Jennifer walked fast and talked faster, as she usually did when she was wound up. "Because," she continued, "last week Angela from Duluth posted that she thought that my look was too New York. What am I supposed to *do*? I'm trying to stride that fine line between looking fashion-forward and what the Midwest wants." She wanted viewers to like her and identify with her. That's why Jennifer spent countless hours each week poring over the network website and *Homestyle's* social media pages. Viewer opinions definitely affected her choices.

"I thought maybe they would like this nice ice silver," she explained, smoothing a hand down the sleeve of her pale gray silk blouse. She had added a princess-length triple strand of cut-glass beads in a neutral color. Not too "big city" for her viewers, right? Or was it? Her forehead creased with tension as the words rushed out. "You know, like in that movie where they freeze everything?"

Ian Carroll, the show's director, bustled up to her. His short beard, Wayfarer-style glasses, burgundy pullover, and gray winter scarf with matching gray slacks hinted at his fastidious nature. That was a major plus, as far as Jennifer was concerned. He always seemed pulled together, whether it was his clothes, his office, or his attitude. He cared about the big things and the little things, and got them all done. Maybe that's why he had a calming influence on her.

"Jennifer, you don't seem happy," Ian said. "How can we make you happy?"

Forgetting about her wardrobe for the moment, Jennifer let her eyes scan the set. Christmas pervaded the atmosphere of *Homestyle,* but she started to see flaws right away. Her eyes found the Christmas tree near the refrigerator in her TV kitchen. "Oh, my gosh, it's so green…and sad."

"The tree?" Ian asked. He always tried to make sure he understood what she meant before he took action.

Jennifer winced. The tree was definitely an issue for her: a green fir with uninspired green and silver decorations. Green on green wouldn't look good on camera at all. And *why* did it have to be green, one of her least favorite colors?

That wasn't the tree's only failing. "Look, it's also dying on the bottom." She pointed out a few lower branches that were beginning to turn brown. While the brown added contrast, it wasn't exactly an improvement.

Ian raised his voice so the set dressers working around him could hear. "Somebody cheer this tree up, please?"

Letting Ian take care of the tree, Jennifer turned around just as Cynthia wheeled a gingerbread Empire State Building out on a cart.

"Oh, whoa. Whoa, there!" Jennifer said, instantly keying in on a problem. "What's going on with all the toy cars?" The size of the cars was completely wrong next to the majestic building.

"I thought it would be cute," Cynthia said.

"But this is the Empire State Building—it's supposed to be magnificent," Jennifer pointed out.

Cynthia gave her a perplexed look. "But it's just gingerbre—"

"I know," Jennifer cut in. There was no time to

waste. Was she the only one who could see how awful it looked? With a forced smile, she explained, "But the scale, the scale. It's ix-nay on the ars-cay, okay?"

"I'm sorry. You got it," Cynthia said, rolling the display cart away.

Belatedly, Jennifer realized how discouraging her words must have been, so she added, "But good job with everything else."

Ian, who was a master at smoothing ruffled feathers, reassured Cynthia. "Really good. Love it."

"Yeah, really good," Jennifer repeated, feeling slightly guilty. But there was no time to dwell on it. She made an impatient gesture, anxious to get on with the show. At least she knew one thing that was absolutely perfect since she had done the work herself. "Now where's that turkey? I am so excited."

A moment later, a prop man appeared carrying the turkey on a large serving platter.

The food on a TV show like *Homestyle with Jennifer Wade* could not simply look "okay." It had to be perfect for the camera, and perfect food took hours of extra prep work. Jennifer sometimes thought of it as makeup for cuisine. The golden-brown bird coming toward her, heaped with stuffing and nestled on a bed of greens, looked even better than Jennifer had remembered. Her attention to detail had certainly paid off, and she was thrilled to see the results.

"Oh, it's so beautiful. I love—"

The prop man raised the turkey for her to see it better. Then he tripped.

Turkey, dressing, and garnish flew toward her, hit her dead center, and slid down her silk shirt to land on the floor.

A high-pitched "Ahh!" of surprise escaped her lips. Jennifer looked down and took in the scope of the catastrophe: the perfectly browned turkey lying broken on the floor surrounded by a jumble of greens, the prop man trying to gather everything back onto the serving platter, and her own grease-stained blouse, obviously ruined. Why had she decided not to wear a Christmas apron for the show? At least her short black skirt had been spared.

"I'm so sorry, so sorry," the prop man said.

"Oh, no!" Jennifer wailed. She didn't need an apology, she needed a miracle. "I spent an hour and a half on the left thigh alone." Dazed, she tried to step to one side, slipped on the greasy floor, and caught herself on the counter.

In an instant, Ian was beside her, doing damage control.

"Don't worry. We have a backup turkey," the prop man said.

"Oh, no." Jennifer looked down at herself again. The situation seemed hopeless. She breathed faster, trying to fill her lungs with air. Her throat constricted. "Okay, but we don't have a backup shirt, do we?" Her voice rose. "*We don't have a backup shirt!*"

"We do have a backup shirt." Ian motioned to a wardrobe assistant. "Flying in: backup shirt."

Aimee rushed forward, carrying a mallard-green

silk blouse, and held it out to Jennifer, who couldn't help but stare at it aghast.

"That's not the same shirt." Jennifer had tried so hard to prepare a perfect show for her viewers, but her dream of presenting the perfect Christmas on TV was crumbling.

"It's the same shirt, just a different color," Aimee assured her.

"But it's *green*," Jennifer protested, feeling suddenly shaky. "I *hate* green."

"Listen, everything is going to be okay," Ian's soothing voice broke in. "We can spray the backup turkey, and we'll be good."

She could tell he was trying to manage her, but she didn't mind because it was helping. The anxiety dropped a notch, and her heartbeat began to slow down. *Would* things be okay? She gave Ian a melancholy look. "No, it won't be perfect. Everything was supposed to be perfect," she fretted. "It's the holiday special."

"No, no, no, it'll totally be perfect," Ian said with a confident smile. He turned and shouted to the crew. "Okay people, let's prep that backup turkey!"

Aimee put a comforting arm around her as they walked back to Jennifer's dressing room to change.

In the end, despite the mishaps, the taping of the show went so well that Jennifer wore a broad smile as they shot the final scene in her *Homestyle* "dining room." She held the beautiful turkey up for the camera before placing it at the center of a table set with taupe stoneware plates and bowls, red tapers in clear candlesticks, and simple crystal stemware. The rest of the meal was arrayed around the turkey: colorful mixed vegetables, salad, cranberry sauce, and whipped butternut squash. She wished she could have spent some time staining the turkey a bit darker, maybe putting a sheen on it with some oil and a blowtorch.

"Mm. It looks so delicious. I just can't wait to eat that turkey," she said. Of course, she didn't want to eat this *actual* turkey, which, like most stage turkeys, was mostly raw and only enhanced and "styled" to look good in photography. But a real holiday turkey like her mom used to cook sounded wonderful.

Clasping her hands in front of her, Jennifer looked directly into the camera and spoke to her viewers. "Thank you so much for joining me on my Christmas special. I'm Jennifer Wade, and from all of us at *Homestyle*, we wish you a Christmas to remember."

"And cut!" Ian called.

Jennifer blew out a breath of relief. The show hadn't been perfect, but it had turned out pretty darn well, considering how things had started. She hoped it was good enough to please her viewers.

CHAPTER 2

"That was fabulous. Congratulations." Paula Marshall, Jennifer's friend and agent, bustled down the steps with Jennifer as they headed to Jennifer's dressing room. The holiday season meant that both women were booked up to their eyeballs, so much so that Paula and Jennifer had to talk business as one or both of them rushed from event to event. Jennifer was grateful to have Paula as an advocate. Outgoing, confident, and persuasive, with a warm brown complexion, long dark hair, and a brilliant smile, Paula was a force to be reckoned with.

Jennifer wanted to take Paula's compliment at face value, but she began to second-guess herself. Would her viewers be able to tell that the turkey wasn't flawless? Should she have added more side dishes? Had she given enough tips that would help her audience with their own holiday preparations? She wanted to make sure her agent wasn't just being supportive. "Thanks, Paula, but was it special enough for Christmas?"

"Come on," Paula said, taking Jennifer's arm,

"nobody does Christmas like you do. And your piece is about to come out in *Aroma Magazine*, which means you've got some momentum, and soon, everyone will know who Jennifer Wade is."

By the Kitchen Network's standards, Jennifer's weekly show was a hit and gaining steadily in viewership, though she wasn't exactly a household name like Rachael Ray or Jamie Oliver. But Paula had been her biggest fan, closest confidante, and strongest advocate for more than a decade now, and if Paula had anything to say about it, Jennifer's name and brand would reach a much wider audience in the not-too-distant future.

Jennifer gave her a wry smile. "So, no pressure is what you're saying."

"No pressure," Paula agreed with a laugh. "Tell me you are coming to my party tonight. Bring Brad."

"Come on, Paula." Jennifer wasn't sure why the mention of the handsome sports commentator instantly put her on guard. They'd gone on several dates in the few months since Paula had introduced them, and Brad was enthusiastic about what he called their "power potential." He wanted them to go public as a couple. Jennifer had been married briefly in her twenties to a controlling man who had left her full of self-doubt, and she longed for a true, deep relationship. She just didn't know if Brad was right for her.

As if reading her mind, Paula said, "Oh, I know he's not your ideal man, but he's a very popular sportscaster, and being seen with him will build up your brand." She had amazing instincts when it came to publicity.

Though uncomfortable with this kind of match-making, Jennifer understood that it came from a place of love. Friend Paula's primary goal was for her to be happy, while agent Paula focused on making Jennifer successful. By pairing Brad with Jennifer, Paula was hoping to kill two birds with one stone. Jennifer smiled at her friend as they walked down the long backstage hallway to the dressing room. "I feel like we're in the old country and this is an arranged marriage. No, Paula, I think my 'brand' and I are just going to go home and take a nice hot bath and go to bed. I'm just not feeling very social tonight."

"I know your feelings about the holidays."

"What you mean?" Jennifer asked warily. It was true that from late November through New Year's Day, she existed in a state of almost-constant anxiety, but she did her best to hide it by projecting a sense of holiday cheer. This used to be her favorite time of year. Now she tried to avoid thinking about the reasons she felt such emotional strain at Thanksgiving and Christmas.

"Well, I know they're very hard on you," Paula said.

Jennifer dismissed the idea. "That's just ridiculous. I just did an entire show based on Christmas." They walked into her dressing room.

Paula chuckled. "Well, you just seem to get so stressed out: the music, you don't like eggnog—"

"Who *does* like eggnog?" Jennifer joked as they retrieved their winter coats from the coatrack.

Paula's eyebrows raised in surprise. "Well, *I* do."

"Yeah, right…" Jennifer said skeptically, but she knew she was dodging the real issue. As they put on their coats, she admitted, "No, you know, to be honest, it's just…my mom made Christmas so special, and she was so wonderful at it." She looked at a framed photo that sat on her dressing table: her mother with short, brown hair and a smile that could light up a room, and herself with all the confidence of a twenty-something girl who could take on the world. The two of them had always faced life together. Doing the best show possible every week was one of the ways Jennifer honored the memory of her mom, who had taught her so much about cooking, decorating, family, and making a home.

Jennifer sighed. She was fortunate to have good friends, but she *missed* being part of a family. And Christmastime held so many reminders of her mother. "Since she's been gone, it just hasn't been the same for me, but…it'll be fine."

Paula studied her face for a moment and then said with absolute certainty, "You know your show is going to be a huge success, and it's going to reach millions of people."

Jennifer gave her a grateful smile—not at the suggestion of fame, but because Paula believed in her and would do anything to help her succeed. Jennifer took comfort in the other woman's strong show of friendship.

They headed out of the building into the brisk air. Near the door of the network building, a TV screen embedded in the wall was already showing teaser clips of the *Homestyle* holiday show. Not so long ago, Jennifer had been a barely known blogger. Now her face was everywhere. Here in New York, clerks in shops or people on the street recognized her now and asked for her autograph. She'd worked hard for that recognition.

Her success came with a price, though. Day in and day out, she attended public events, did TV, radio, and web interviews, planned and wrote her TV show, supervised her blog and social media. The work was never-ending. Still, it filled her life with purpose and left no time to feel sorry for herself.

Paula said, "If you come to my party, you won't have to do anything for a whole week."

"You're serious?" Jennifer wondered if she had heard correctly. Although Paula the friend was always supportive, Paula the agent almost never suggested taking time off. A week of complete freedom was an enticing prospect.

"Yes," Paula said as they walked toward the taxi stand. "Listen, I have the most gorgeous, gorgeous chalet near Aspen. Go there. Total peace and quiet. You'll love it. And it's right next to the best hiking trails that you can imagine."

"Hiking." Jennifer nearly laughed out loud. Outdoor activities weren't a selling point for her. "Paula, this is *me* you're talking to."

"I know, right?" Paula said. "But it's also a stone's throw away from the best spa."

That caught Jennifer's attention. "Well, I do love a good spa." Paula was perceptive and had an uncanny way of knowing what Jennifer needed, sometimes even before Jennifer realized it. It was just one of the reasons she was such a good friend.

"Uh-huh. Sometimes you just got to forget about everything and get away." Paula smiled as if she could see that Jennifer was going to take the bait.

Jennifer had been feeling pressure building for weeks leading up to her Christmas special. The special was done now, but Christmas was still coming, and Jennifer knew her tension would get worse until after the holidays were over. The gift of a whole week of relaxation was too good to pass up. As they reached the taxi stand, she said, "All right. Thank you, Paula. That's an amazingly generous offer."

"Ah, stop—it's the least I can do. Now you come to my party tonight, and bring Brad."

Jennifer got into the taxi, chuckling at her friend's negotiating tactics. Party with Brad. That was the bargain, and Jennifer always kept her commitments. "Well, I guess I *have* to now."

"You do," Paula agreed. "I'll see you later."

"Bye," Jennifer said, still smiling. The thought of getting away from it all made the prospect of going to a party tonight more agreeable. In fact, she was starting to feel some actual holiday cheer.

CHAPTER 3

D r. John Blake only had a few house calls left for the day. As he drove, surrounded by the beauty of nature in Colorado's high country, he couldn't help but think how fortunate he was to live here. He braked suddenly as a squirrel darted across the road in front of his pickup, and then grinned as he watched it scamper off to the side. He and his children loved watching animals so much that he'd made a squirrel feeder in the shape of a small picnic table for their backyard. He started down the road again, glad that he had four-wheel drive and antilock brakes—although in truth, up here in the high country, those things weren't so much a luxury as a necessity.

He headed back toward North Creek, Colorado, population 4,820, where he had been born and raised. Maneuvering through the heart of town, he waved to people on the street as he passed. Nearly everyone in North Creek knew everyone else. It had the perfect blend of small-town feeling and larger-town tourist amenities, with skiing and snowboarding in the winter, hiking and fishing in the summer, and festivals and cute shops year-round.

Activating his blinker, he looked in all directions before turning onto one of North Creek's secondary roads. He was safety-minded. *Might as well do all you can to protect yourself from things you can control when there are so many things you can't.*

A flash of sweet sorrow at the memory made him catch his breath. He shook off the urge to let his thoughts wander. It was Christmas, and he had good work to do. There weren't many people in the world who had jobs they enjoyed so much and the kind of deep connections he had with his patients and their families.

He pulled the truck up in front of the house of his next appointment and checked the clock on his phone. Good, he was running a few minutes early. He had plenty of time to spend. He never liked to leave a family feeling worried or shortchanged because he'd had to leave in a hurry. He thought of his patient, little Katy. Hopefully, there was nothing seriously wrong with her.

As he got out of the pickup, he grabbed his black leather medical bag, one of his few nods to formality in medicine. Life in Colorado's mountains was more casual than in big cities. Today he wore a brown leather jacket with shearling collar and cuffs over a quilted vest and a fleece with a pair of comfortable jeans. As a Colorado native, he knew that layering his clothes was the trick to keeping warm. No hat or gloves today, but he always kept those in the truck for occasions when he was going to spend a long time outside.

The house was white, with red trim around the windows, surrounded by a wooden picket fence. A waving inflatable Santa stood in the front yard beside a bird feeder. A wide front porch that ran the entire width of the house was decorated for Christmas. Fir garlands accented with frosted red bows and tiny clear lights lined the porch rails, and strings of colored bulbs draped the row of spindly balusters above the porch frame.

John knocked beside the glass on the front door. Nancy Varney, a short, kindly-looking woman with graying brown hair and rimless glasses, answered the door.

"Nancy, how are you doing?" he asked.

"Dr. Blake, thank you so much for coming. Katy just doesn't seem herself," Nancy said in a rush. She opened the door wider for him to come in.

"Well, let's take a look at the little patient." John walked into the living room and saw Katy huddled on a cushion on a rattan chair. "There she is."

"I guess I'm just a nervous mom," Nancy said, looking for all the world like the librarian she was. She fiddled anxiously with the strand of pearls visible at the neck of her cream ruffled blouse and purple sweater.

Katy, his feline patient, was a chocolate-point, doll-faced Himalayan. John approached Katy slowly, holding out his hand to her and speaking in soft tones. The blue-eyed cat sniffed him.

"How are you doing, sweetie? Let's take a look here," John said, gently stroking Katy's forehead with the backs of his fingers.

"This morning Katy tried to jump onto the curio cabinet, but she slipped and fell," Nancy explained. "She hasn't been herself since then, and she limps when she walks."

John had Nancy hold Katy while he examined her. He shared his findings as he worked. "She's alert and responsive. That's always good. Temperature and heart rate just slightly elevated. Her coat looks healthy, and you're doing a great job with the grooming." He felt along the cat's neck and stomach. "No lumps or enlarged lymph nodes. Okay, let's see how she walks."

Nancy put Katy on the floor, went to the other side of the room, and called her. The cat gingerly hobbled over to her.

John nodded. "She's definitely limping on that right hind leg, but she is using it. That's encouraging."

Nancy picked Katy up, and John examined each of the cat's legs, starting at the foot and working his way up. He saved the injured leg for last.

Katy flinched and gave a short *waowrr* when he touched it.

"It's tender, isn't it, sweetie? I'm sorry. We'll get you fixed up," he said in a soothing voice. Then he told Nancy, "The leg is warm and sensitive right now. It's a sprain, but we can treat it right here at home."

Nancy looked relieved.

John gave Katy a shot of Meloxidyl. "This is just a low dose of anti-inflammatory to help with the pain."

Nancy made them a pot of tea, and they sat while John explained how to care for Katy's leg injury.

"She needs to be kept quiet for a week or so—no energetic playing with string and no jumping. If she doesn't start to feel better within a few days, we may need to do an X-ray, but we'd have to take her to Boulder for that. Don't worry. I think this will clear up pretty quickly." John took a long sip of hot tea. "A little bit of rest is all she needs. Katy is going to be just fine."

"How are your kids?" Nancy asked. She held Katy still on her lap, petting her.

John brightened. He loved to talk about his children. "Good. Jamie is reading every book she can get her hands on, Kyle wants to be a vet just like his old man, and Daisy is…Daisy."

Nancy nodded with understanding. "Have you decided what to do about your practice?"

"Well, I've got my eye on a spot in town where I'm thinking of setting up my office," John said. He didn't like the idea of adding monthly rent to his expenses, but a town the size of North Creek needed a physical veterinary facility that could handle surgery. For a few years, he had mostly been making house calls and seeing an occasional patient at his house, but his practice had outgrown the tiny home office.

"What about the barn where your wife kept her horses?" Nancy asked.

John felt a pang at the reminder of Julie. It had only been three years since he and the kids lost her.

Sometimes the pain of that loss still felt fresh—usually in the evening after the kids had gone to bed.

John and Julie had met in her hometown of Fort Collins while he was in veterinary school and she was an undergrad. Julie loved horses, and many of their dates involved horseback riding. Once when he was on call, Julie had actually helped John deliver a foal. After they moved to North Creek, having a barn at their home had allowed her to buy Aragorn, an Arabian chestnut gelding. She had supplemented their income by boarding other horses and giving riding lessons.

Everything about the barn brought back happy memories of his petite blonde wife—Julie mucking out the stalls, grooming Aragorn, storing massive bales of hay for neighboring ranchers, teaching Jamie to ride. The building represented all those happy times to John. If he cleared Julie's gear out of the barn and gave the place a different purpose, might he lose some of those precious memories? His heart couldn't risk it. The barn was too important.

"Such a beautiful old building," Nancy said.

"Yeah, it is. It's just… I'm not sure I'm ready yet." For a moment, he was lost in thought. Then he said, "Well, I'd better get going. I've got a few more house calls to make."

"What do I owe you for today?" Nancy asked.

John shook his head with a smile. "No charge—it's Christmas."

Chapter 4

That evening, Jennifer arranged to meet Brad at Paula's place for the party. She had learned that arriving separately avoided a lot of awkwardness at the end of a date, especially with a man she was just dating casually, despite Paula's urging for them to get more serious. Jennifer and Brad took separate taxis and arrived at Paula's apartment building at the same time.

They rode up the elevator together looking like the perfect couple. Jennifer was dressed all in black, in an understated lace minidress with a sheer mesh panel at the neckline and scalloped lace at the hem, topped with a soft, drapey blazer that was nearly as long as her dress. The short dress and stiletto pumps showed off her legs, while the blazer kept her warm in the wintery weather and flowed with her. She had put on evening makeup and wore her blonde hair down in loose curls. All in all, her outfit was festive but comfortable. Brad was dressed for success in a dark suit with a light-blue spread-collared shirt and maroon tie.

Paula's apartment was amazingly roomy, especially

for Manhattan, with plenty of space for Paula's many party guests to spread out. The decor was stylish, modern, and monochromatic, in shades of white and black. Light hardwood floors, broad expanses of wall, and floor-to-ceiling windows added to the impression of space. A fire blazed in the gas log fireplace, in front of which a glass-and-chrome coffee table sat on a cream flokati rug. Near the living room, glass doors opened to a terrace that had a spectacular view of the city.

The ultramodern kitchen had long white work surfaces, stainless appliances, and open shelving. The kitchen was completely open to the living room, and a beige counter that ran the length of the room could be used as a dining table or as a bar. Tonight, it was a bar. Jennifer got a flute of champagne, and Brad picked up a glass of white wine. At the end of the bar, a silvery-white faux Christmas tree sparkled with clear fairy lights. They chatted as they walked around the apartment.

Jennifer was nervous as she told Brad that she was going away for a week. She wasn't quite sure why. Was she afraid to rock the boat in their relationship? Even if Brad wasn't her ideal, and their connection was somewhat tepid, he was a savvy, romantic choice.

"You're going to Colorado," Brad said, sounding disappointed. "I was hoping we'd go to all the holiday parties here in New York." Brad was zealous about networking and determined to break out of local news into national sportscasting. He'd set his sights on a job at ESPN. He'd admitted to Jennifer that he wanted to be seen with her in public as much as possible so they would be known as a power couple.

Jennifer was sorry to disappoint him, but she was looking forward to escaping the stresses and frenetic activity of New York City. Although she sometimes found the pace invigorating, part of her also yearned for a simpler environment that would let her balance her thriving career with...with what? She wasn't sure, and she needed some quiet time to think about it, so she tried to explain. "I'm sorry, Brad, but when Paula offered me her cabin... I don't know... It's just, if I can't get away for the holidays, when can I? I work the other fifty-one weeks of the year."

Fortunately, he wasn't a controlling person like her ex. Brad shrugged. "I understand. It's just—don't take too long. Between your career and my career, we'd be unstoppable."

Jennifer smiled and nodded. She liked Brad just fine. He was friendly, handsome, outgoing, and passionate about his work. She knew that he, in turn, was impressed with her success, and he often told her she was beautiful. He seemed to have a real affection for her, but they weren't exactly in love. She knew he was right, though: together, they would draw media attention both in the sports world and from the *Homestyle* audience. But it felt...artificial. Uncomfortable. A faint reminder that her ex, Ashton, had used her to advance his career. She didn't blame Brad at all for being ambitious, though. Success was important to her, as well. She just didn't see it as a good enough basis for a relationship.

She'd all but given up on finding a soul mate. With Ashton, she had believed she was truly in love—only to learn after they'd married that he was far different in reality from the man she had thought him to be. It had been a devastating experience. After the divorce, Jennifer had taken refuge in her work.

Paula, in a black turtleneck sweater dress and silver jacket, came up to welcome them. "Ooh, wow. Honey, you look gorgeous."

Jennifer thanked her. As a hostess, Paula was obviously in her element, circulating among her guests, chatting and making introductions, and keeping everything running smoothly. Jennifer enjoyed watching her.

Paula turned to Brad. "And Brad, you look as handsome as always."

He sketched a bow of thanks and said, "Milady."

"I am so glad that you came and you came together," Paula said. Jennifer could almost hear her friend thinking, *See? You make a great-looking couple.*

"Thank you, Paula," Jennifer said. "Your party is amazing, and you and your apartment—but especially you—look stunning."

"Thank you." Paula turned to Brad again. "Can I borrow her?"

He smiled and nodded, then held up a finger. "But just for a minute."

Paula steered Jennifer away. "Come with me and

allow me to introduce you to the network president. He's right over here by the crudités."

Jennifer spoke with the president of the Kitchen Network, feeling awkward at first. She started off the conversation with business, but once she got him on the subject of his grandchildren, he grew very animated. They ended up talking for nearly an hour. Jennifer reminded herself that this kind of casual chat in a nonbusiness setting was exactly why Paula had wanted her here. She moved on to mingle with more of the guests.

Brad spent the last part of the party chatting up a sexy young producer from ESPN. Jennifer wasn't jealous. He was just hoping to improve his chances of getting a job there. But even if he'd been outrageous in his flirting, Jennifer didn't think it would have bothered her. They hadn't made any commitment to each other. Their careers were on a similar upward trajectory, but other than that, they didn't seem to have much in common.

Parties weren't always fun for Jennifer. She often busied herself in activities like straightening the buffet, clearing dishes, or cleaning. It was comforting. It reminded her of helping her friend Meredith with her catering business.

The clock had crept well past midnight when Brad went home and the caterers left. Jennifer stayed behind, cleaning up and stacking dishes in the dishwasher.

Paula said goodbye to her last few guests at the

door and then returned to the kitchen. She looked chagrinned. "What are you doing?"

Jennifer smiled. "I'm cleaning your kitchen. You've got so much here. Come on, you can't do it all alone." As far as she was concerned, helping to clean up was just good manners.

"No, stop," Paula said. "As of now, you are officially on vacation."

Jennifer picked up a few more dishes and loaded them into the dishwasher.

Paula said, "Make that your last batch. Come on, I want you to have a drink with me. Just leave all this."

Reluctantly, Jennifer went to the long table that fronted the kitchen and sat on a beige upholstered chair. She hated to leave a mess. She sighed. "Christmas is so much work. Christmas comes with a 'stick.'"

"But you are so good at it," Paula said. "And people like us, we don't know how to do anything else but make it perfect."

Jennifer watched as her friend poured them each a glass of pinot blanc. Paula was right, of course. They both wanted every detail of a project to be *just so*. Even their perpetually tidy apartments were examples of their attention to detail, although Paula's was spare and modern, while her own was full of homey touches. Perfectionism had a cost, though. Jennifer felt a constant pressure to do more, to improve. The price was that she never stopped to simply enjoy the *now*.

"When was the last time that it didn't feel like

work—that it felt like a *real* Christmas?" Jennifer asked.

"Oh." Paula chuckled and put her wine glass down. "Well, m'darlin. If I tell you that, then I'll be telling you my age."

"You know, I remember this one Christmas," Jennifer said, "when my mom sewed me this special dress—I was playing an angel in the Christmas pageant at church—and it was all sparkly and glowing, almost iridescent. I loved it so much I didn't want to take it off, even when we got home. So she let me fall asleep on the couch waiting for Santa. I fell asleep with the sound of Christmas music, the smell of gingerbread, and the feeling of her hand on my hair..."

Reliving the memory, she felt her throat tighten, and tears threatened to fall as she said, "It was so magical. And I just don't know if Christmas is ever going to feel like that again—not this pressure to be perfect, just the simple magic of Christmas."

Being the only child of a single mom might've seemed like a disadvantage to some people, but Jennifer's mother had managed to make their family of two feel complete. Christmas had been *their* holiday. The two of them had decorated the house to Christmas music playing on their stereo. They'd shopped for groceries together. When money was tight, they'd had to be creative. Her mother had often said, "Make something out of what you have." They'd gone window shopping for ideas. They'd baked and made homemade gifts for friends and neighbors.

Jennifer had always dreamed of passing those traditions on to her own children. She wanted to see the magic of Christmas through their eyes. But she'd never had kids. It was one of her regrets. So instead, she showed her viewers how to make their own homes and families feel special. At their core, her shows, articles, and blogs had all been inspired by her amazing mother.

"You know, your mom sounds like she was a wonderful woman," Paula said. "And maybe you can have it that way again: simple and perfect."

Jennifer held up her wine glass in a toast. "Here's to my mom, who made Christmas magical."

Paula clinked her glass against Jennifer's. "To your mom."

Reluctantly, Jennifer stood up and said, "I should be going. If I'm going to get to Colorado in the morning, I have to pack."

"Yes, you do!" Paula's genuine excitement for Jennifer was contagious.

"I'll call you when I get there," Jennifer promised, giving her friend a hug. "Thank you!"

CHAPTER 5

Was there anything more uncomfortable than a first date? John despised them.

Aiming for somewhere between casual and dressy, he'd worn a black dress shirt with the collar unbuttoned and black jeans. He'd chosen a nice restaurant in a reasonable price range, decorated in what the owner called "Grandma's house shabby chic." Julie would've laughed at that description since she'd claimed that everything that started out new in their house eventually ended up "shabby chic"—thanks to the kids.

White fairy lights lined the windows of the restaurant inside. Soft jazz renditions of Christmas music played on the sound system.

John looked across the table at his date, Brooke Hanson, the first woman he'd been out with since Julie died. Brooke had been his classmate in high school. They'd both been popular, but he'd been studious—a sort of jock-nerd—while she'd hung out with cliques of fashion-conscious party goers. Their paths had only crossed at football games. Now, though, she was one of the few single women in town his age, so he'd finally relented and let his friends Stan and Holly Barbour set them up. Stan and Holly were such romantics that they wanted everyone to be happy and in love. But John already regretted agreeing to this date. It just didn't feel right.

"Well, this is nice," Brooke said.

"It is. It's nice," he said, hoping she couldn't tell how uncomfortable he felt. He wondered if Brooke felt that way, too. He was certainly struggling to make small talk. Had it always been this hard?

Brooke took a sip of her wine. "I just can't believe we've never been on a date before."

Fumbling for a reply, John took a gulp from his wine glass, too. "Hm."

"Because, you know," Brooke went on, with a nervous-sounding laugh, "I had a crush on you in high school."

She *had*? John felt a strange mixture of surprise and embarrassment. "Uh, no, I definitely didn't know." High school seemed like a lifetime ago.

Brooke gave him a look of disbelief. "Oh, come on."

"I-I didn't," John stammered, shaking his head. Although she had been pretty enough to catch his eye back then, they hadn't seemed to have much in common, so he had never asked her out.

"But you were the quarterback, and I was the cheerleader. We should have been a couple."

When she put it that way, it did seem obvious, John thought. "I guess so."

"Then you got married," Brooke went on, "and then she—"

John froze. It was jarring to hear her chatter blithely about his marriage when he still missed Julie so much. And now he couldn't help but compare Julie's generous, caring, and easy manner with Brooke's thoughtlessness and forced conversation.

Brooke seemed to notice her mistake. She cleared her throat. "I'm sorry. I don't know why I brought that up."

"It's okay. It's all right," John said, trying to put her at ease. But he wasn't sure that it *was* all right. The strain of making conversation was even greater now. Trying to cut the tension, he began, "So how's—"

"So how was your burger?" Brooke asked at the same time.

"My burger is…it was good. It was fine," he replied, still stumbling over small talk. "How's your tofu?"

"Do you want some?" Brooke offered. "You should try it."

Tofu did not sound appetizing at all. John had tried bean curd a few times and found it flavorless and either slimy or spongy, depending on how it was served. So tofu fell into his life-is-too-short category of foods. He held out a hand to forestall Brooke. "Oh no, I really don't like tof—" he began.

She held out a forkful right in front of him. What could he do? He couldn't refuse without looking like a jerk. With resignation, he accepted the bite and chewed.

"It's good, right?" she said, waiting for his reaction.

Good was not a word he could honestly use to describe the tofu. He didn't like it. At all. But he couldn't very well say so without hurting her feelings. John searched for something to say that wouldn't sound rude. "Mm-hm. It's, uh…interesting consistency," he said, still chewing. It was the best he could do on the spur of the moment.

Brooke's expression fell. "It's nice," she said, but her smile did not return. She looked away, drew a deep breath, and sighed.

John signaled for the waitress to bring the check. He didn't want to make Brooke feel bad, but he did hope to wrap up the date fairly quickly. She must be able to see by now that they weren't well matched. Stan and Holly would be disappointed that John and Brooke hadn't hit it off. It hadn't been a total loss, though. The evening had told John what he needed to know: Brooke was not right for him.

When he finished paying the bill, John helped Brooke put on her winter coat. At the truck, he held the door for her as she got in. Most of the five-minute drive to her house was silent. Still, as a gentleman, he was determined to finish the date as pleasantly as possible. He helped her out of the truck, walked her to the door of her small bungalow, and thanked her for having a meal with him.

Getting out her key, Brooke gave him a flirtatious look. "Would you like to come in?"

He felt his face flush. She wasn't making this easy on him. "Uh, no, thank you. I need to be getting home."

"All right." She blinked in disappointment and looked up at him through her lashes. "But...we can't end the evening without a good-night kiss, can we?"

That was exactly what he had hoped to do.

She leaned toward him.

He gave Brooke a swift peck on the cheek and fled back to his truck.

John pulled his pickup into the driveway of his snow-covered house, a lovely home built of light-colored wood logs in a modern mountain-rustic style. He parked and went inside to his children's rooms to tuck them in and kiss them good night. White Christmas lights were strung along the walls and across the room that Daisy and Kyle shared. John hadn't done much holiday decorating again this year, but the kids loved the little clear lights, so he had let them choose where to put them up. He gave Daisy a kiss on the forehead. Kyle had fallen asleep on top of his quilt, so John lifted him up and tucked him under the covers.

When John got to Jamie's room, she was still awake, reading a mystery book by the light of a headlamp that perched on her forehead just above her glasses. He wasn't upset that she was still awake. It was a sweet reminder that she was her mother's daughter. Julie had often read at bedtime, sometimes getting so wrapped up in a book that she didn't realize how late it was.

"Guess who should be asleep and not reading at this hour?" he said in a teasing tone.

"Dad, I'm just trying to finish this chapter." This was a familiar bedtime conversation. No matter where Jamie was in her current book, she always wanted to read just a little bit more. If he left it up to her, she would read for hours longer.

"You're going to have to finish the chapter tomorrow. Really," he said, taking the book from her and putting it down. "Yes, the suspense will keep you awake. Take your light off please."

She pulled the headlamp from her head and fumbled to turn it off.

He took it gently from her. "I'll figure it out. You get in bed."

She removed her glasses and put them on the table by her bed.

"All right, young lady. Nighty-night," he said, pulling up the quilt and tucking it in around her.

"Night-night," she murmured.

"Sweet dreams, okay? Love you."

John shut the door to the bedroom softly, jogged down the stairs, deposited Jamie's headlamp on the dish-covered kitchen island, and began cleaning up.

He always thought of Julie when he was in the kitchen. She had loved cooking, and they had always enjoyed the quiet companionship of cleaning up together. Now there was just the quiet. If it weren't for

Julie's parents, who lived close by, and his best friend Dan, who came over regularly, that loneliness might have overwhelmed him. Even though his own parents and grandparents had passed long ago, his life was full of friends and family and blessings.

As if on cue, Dan Daniels opened the back door and came in. Dan was in his late fifties, with fluffy gray hair and a beard that managed to look bushy even at a medium length. Biscuit, the Blakes's border terrier mix rescue dog, met him at the door.

"Hey, Biscuit."

"Dan!" John greeted him.

Dan took off his hat and parka, revealing a fisherman's chunky-knit cardigan underneath, and hung them on the rack near the door. "John. What did you make for dinner?" He made his way over to the stove and groaned with dismay. "Aw, stroganoff again?"

"Bunny made it. It's simple. The kids love it," John explained, then teased his friend. "You don't like it, I got some kibble you could help yourself to."

Dan dismissed the mock threat. "I'll take the strog." He picked up a fork, ate a bite of stroganoff straight out of the pot, and chewed contemplatively.

When John finished cleaning the kitchen, they adjourned to the backgammon table in the next room. Dan carried the pot with him and continued eating while they played.

"Double sixes!" John said, putting down the dice cup. "*Again*."

"For the love of Pete," Dan groused good-naturedly around a mouthful of stroganoff. "So how'd things go with what's-her-name?"

"Oh," John said. "Well, she force-fed me tofu."

"Ew," Dan commiserated.

"Yeah, it wasn't a good fit," John replied. "I don't really like being set up, anyway, to tell you the truth. I think these things should happen naturally and organically, come together easily, like two pieces of a puzzle."

He and Julie had fit together from the start. He had been working in a training clinic one morning when a petite blonde girl walked in carrying an injured seventy-pound yellow Labrador retriever.

"Pixie's been hit by a car," she'd explained. Throughout the examination, Julie had refused to leave Pixie's side, obviously terrified her pet would not recover.

John's heart had contracted with pain for her. His instincts had always been to ease suffering, which was one reason he had gone into veterinary medicine. But he'd felt a particularly urgent need to help Julie.

To keep her mind off her fear, he'd struck up a conversation with her. During X-rays and blood analysis and various other tests, they'd talked for more than an hour. He'd learned she was an undergrad studying for a business degree and lived at home with her parents to save money. That had led to a discussion about family and animals and what an important part their pets played in their families.

Finally, John had been able to assure Julie that

Pixie's injuries were limited to torn ligaments and a broken leg, which he could repair surgically.

Julie had cried with relief and hugged John. He had already been drawn to her, and her love for her dog had made the attraction even stronger.

Pixie had come through the surgery with flying colors. Afterward, John had offered to come by and check on her for the first week, and Julie had gladly accepted. John and Julie had gradually gotten to know each other and had begun to date.

Because they'd been students, most of their dates were simple. They had studied together, ridden horses, hiked, and gone on picnics. After Pixie's leg had improved, they'd taken her hiking with them. And they'd talked, always talked. Everything about being with her had felt so natural, so right.

John wondered if he'd ever love like that again.

Dan rattled the backgammon dice in the cup and rolled them, pulling John back to the present. Dan gave a satisfied grunt. "Double fives. I'll take it." He moved his checker and took another bite of stroganoff. "Your turn."

John rolled the dice.

CHAPTER 6

Jennifer looked forward to the drive from Denver International Airport up to Aspen. Taught by her mom, she'd gotten her driver's license during high school, like Meredith and most of her other friends in New Jersey had. Jennifer was a good driver, but living in New York, she didn't get to do it very often anymore. She missed it. Long drives alone refreshed her and helped clear her mind.

Her travel day hadn't started out well. Her flight to Denver had been delayed. Then it had been canceled altogether, and all of the people on her plane had been rebooked on flights later in the day. She'd ended up in a middle seat toward the back of the plane.

In Denver, after waiting at the baggage carousel for half an hour, she'd discovered that her luggage had been put on an earlier flight and was in a holding area. By the time she reached the car rental counter, she was frustrated and in a hurry. She hadn't even considered spending a night in Denver, especially since she had intended to arrive much earlier in the day. And a posh, private chalet awaited her. At this point, she didn't want to waste another minute of the luxurious vacation Paula had promised her.

"Jennifer Wade," the car rental agent said. He gave her a questioning look.

"Yes, *that* Jennifer Wade, yes," she acknowledged. She was used to being recognized in New York.

But the rental agent's face did not register any recognition. Maybe she wasn't as recognizable here as she was in New York, where her likeness was plastered on billboards. He consulted his computer terminal. "Yup, we've got a nice four-wheel-drive SUV for you."

That didn't sound very fun to Jennifer at all. A clunky old SUV? She'd been hoping for something a bit more luxurious or sleek to start off her vacation. "Ooh, do you have anything a little faster?" she asked. "I was hoping I could get there before it's too dark."

The clerk hesitated. "An SUV would be a great choice in this weather."

She smiled one of her patented Jennifer Wade smiles that always got her what she wanted. It was an expression of friendly determination with a flash of challenge in her eyes. Paula called that smile "velvet over steel."

The rental agent sighed. "Well, there are a couple of options I could show you. Will you be needing to rent a GPS today?"

Jennifer held up her smartphone for him to see. "Everything I need is in here."

The clerk smiled wanly and clicked something on

his computer. He printed out her rental agreement, and it took an exasperating amount of time to complete it—sheesh, there was a waiver for turning down the GPS?

It was late afternoon and snowing by the time she pulled out of the rental car lot. The weather had turned the skies gloomy. And it was rush hour. The silver sports coupe she had chosen crawled along I-70 heading west through Denver. The sun was low on the horizon, nearly blinding her. She flipped down her visor and put on a pair of sunglasses.

"What time does the sun set today?" she asked the electronic assistant on her telephone.

"The sun will set at 4:38 pm today," the electronic voice answered.

She blew out an annoyed breath. The last thing she wanted was to be wandering around in the dark looking for an unfamiliar place. When she had asked the car rental agent for directions, he had told her, "It's a straight shot on I-70 for hours. Then there are lots of signs—you can't miss it."

But she *might* miss it, especially if it was dark and snowing. Well, at least no one was at the chalet waiting for her. There were no engagements, no deadlines, nothing to do but relax. She didn't have to worry about disappointing anyone by arriving late, and Paula had told her she didn't need to call right away. So why was she worrying?

"You're a grownup," she chided herself. "You can handle a freeway and following a bunch of signs.

Besides, you've got the GPS on your phone." On the far side of Denver, the traffic finally started to ease up, and she gladly accelerated to the posted speed limit as the road climbed into the foothills. "Straight shot for hours," she reminded herself.

She felt the tense knot between her shoulder blades getting tighter. When she tried to massage her neck and shoulders with one hand, she bumped the steering wheel, started to drift out of her lane, and yanked the wheel back straight. The tires of the impractical sports coupe slipped on the road. Her stomach clenched, and she held her breath. The back of the car slewed to the right for a few seconds. She steered into the skid, and the car straightened out again. *That was close*, she thought. She made herself start breathing again.

"Okay, Colorado, you'd better be worth it." It was getting dark. Snow swirled around the rental car. "I can't see anything," she muttered and took off her sunglasses.

What she really needed right now was something to take her mind off the long drive. Maybe she could listen to some music or news. She turned on the car radio. Since she didn't know any of the local stations, she tried the preset buttons. The first station was playing Christmas music. She listened for a few seconds, but then her mind went back to the Christmas special she had just finished shooting, and she thought of the different ways she could have set the table that would have displayed the food to better advantage.

No, she would be better off not listening to

Christmas music at the moment. Even though the holidays held good thoughts of her mother, it had only been two years since Jennifer lost her, and Christmas music felt like an unfair reminder that she had lost all of the family that she'd had left in the world. Not all of her friends, of course, but all of her family. She tried another preset button. This station played Christmas hymns. She tried a third button, but only found more Christmas music. In frustration, she shut the radio off. She glanced down at her GPS and saw she was perfectly on course. She gave a sigh. With nothing else to occupy her mind, the memories came.

Her thoughts inadvertently drifted back to when she was in her twenties. While putting herself through the Institute of Culinary Education in New York, she'd frequently helped her friend Meredith with catering jobs. During one of these catering events, Jennifer had met Ashton Randall III at his parents' elegant Long Island home. He had enigmatic hazel eyes, patrician features, an aquiline nose, short copper hair, and lips curled into a perpetual smirk.

After the party, he'd offered to take her home. The rest, as they say, was history—bad history.

After a couple of months of formal courtship, Ashton had proposed, and Jennifer had accepted. What she had wanted most was a real family: children, a home, and a sense of belonging. Only much later had Jennifer realized that the warning signs with Ashton had been there all along. It had taken years to recognize that he viewed her as little more than an ornament, a pretty tool to use in furthering his position and prestige. In his narcissism, he had tried to control every part of her life.

Looking back now, Jennifer decided that the best thing to come out of those wasted years had been her blog, which had ultimately led to her friendship with Paula and to her career. Maybe she would give Paula a call, after all, as soon as she got to the chalet.

Jennifer pressed down harder on the gas pedal of her sports coupe.

CHAPTER 7

John used extra caution driving the GMC 4X4 through the snow toward Stan and Holly Barbour's ranch. One of their horses was having a difficult labor, so they had called John, and John had brought his son. Kyle, who claimed he wanted to be a vet, loved going on house calls with his dad. Normally, John wouldn't have taken him out after bedtime, but the Christmas holidays had started, and Kyle didn't have school the next day.

"You tired, buddy?" John asked Kyle.

Kyle rubbed his eyes and yawned. "No."

John had to smile at that. In most cases, Kyle said exactly what he was thinking, but he wouldn't admit to being tired. He didn't want to lose out on spending extra time with his dad. John could understand that, but he wanted to make sure Kyle didn't feel like he had to be interested in veterinary medicine just to get his attention. "You don't have to come on these house calls with me if you don't want to."

"No, I want to," Kyle insisted. "I'm your *assistant*."

"The best," John agreed. "Okay. Have you thought about what you might want to be when you grow up—other than a vet? You could be almost anything, you know. You have plenty of time to plan."

"I know," Kyle said. "Can't I be an animal doctor like you?"

"Sure," John said. But Kyle was only seven, and John wanted to make sure his son was prepared for what he might see tonight. John and Kyle climbed out of the truck, both dressed in layers against the cold. "I need to warn you, buddy. I've seen some breech births go wrong, and in those cases, the mare or foal can die. You need to be prepared, okay?"

Kyle nodded. "But we'll try to save them." His son's endless optimism was one of the things that kept John afloat.

Stan met them at the barn door. "Thanks for coming down with the storm coming in," he said.

"How's she doing?" John asked.

"Not so good. It's a breech for sure," Stan said.

"Your mare is having a foal," Kyle said, demonstrating his knowledge of the situation.

"That's right," Stan said. "It's a good thing your dad's here."

John looked down at Kyle. "Let's get to it. You ready, buddy?" He opened the stall and spoke in soothing tones to the palomino mare. "Good, she's standing. That's what we need during a breech delivery. First things first, though. What's the first step, Buddy?"

"We wash up," Kyle said.

"Exactly," John answered. "We have to be fast but clean." All of them disinfected their hands and arms at a deep sink in the next stall. They quickly wrapped the mare's tail to keep it out of the way and then cleaned the hind end of the mare.

As they worked, John recalled the time Julie had helped him deliver a foal. Once when he was on call during veterinary training, they had been interrupted on a movie date by a call for John to assist with a foaling at a nearby farm. Instead of being disappointed, Julie had gone along to help. At the time, he had still been learning about horses, whereas she had grown up riding horses and working in stables, so she'd had far more hands-on experience with them than he had. She had assisted, coached him, and cheered him on through the whole process. Even in the horse stable with her hair messed up and straw sticking to her clothes, she'd looked beautiful to him. When he'd thanked her for being so understanding, she had winked and said, "I wouldn't have missed it for anything. This is where the magic happens."

From then on, every time they'd faced an unexpected situation—a burnt roast, a flat tire, a broken water heater, a baby arriving two weeks early—it had been their private joke to say, "This is where the magic happens." In truth, the magic had been anywhere they were together.

It took John, Kyle, and Stan working together to position the breech foal and bring it out of the mare quickly enough to save it. Then John had to clear away some mucus to get the newborn breathing. It was a difficult, messy process—and deeply satisfying, once the mare and foal were both out of danger.

With the foal safely delivered, John packed up his medical bag. For a breech birth, the process had gone even better than he could have hoped.

"Pretty amazing, right?" he said to Kyle.

"Yeah, it was. And she's going to be okay now. And the foal?" Kyle asked.

"She knows exactly what to do. They're both going to be just fine. Don't you worry," John said. He and Kyle stopped at another stall in the barn to visit Aragorn, the Arabian chestnut gelding that had belonged to Julie. He was well taken care of, and Julie would have loved knowing that Stan and Holly's kids were learning to ride him. The horse nuzzled John's face. Just being near Aragorn made John feel closer to Julie. He blinked away the sting of threatening tears and put his arm around Kyle, pulling him close. They were still petting the gelding's nose when Stan joined them again.

"I was pretty worried before you got here," Stan said. "Hey, John, could I have a word?"

"Of course. Kyle, why don't you head to the truck. I'll be there in a second."

"I hate to do this," Stan said, his voice low and apologetic, "but we're a little bit short right now."

"Stan, don't worry about it," John said. "It's the holidays." Stan and Holly were generous, compassionate people who shared their kindness with a family of six kids, two of whom were adopted. John could well imagine how expensive this time of year was for eight people. And they took such good care of Aragorn.

Stan looked relieved. "I will settle up with you in the new year."

"Okay."

"Thank you, John."

"You got it," John said. He genuinely loved this time of year, and he didn't want his friends to feel any pressure.

"In the meantime," Stan said, "will you take one of Holly's apple pies? She makes the best in the county."

"We would love that," John said. Julie had loved baking—bread, cookies, pies. He missed the aroma. He and the kids would enjoy a fresh homemade pie, especially at this time of year.

As they walked from the barn to the house to pick up the pie, John noticed it was snowing harder now. He would need to be especially careful driving. There were no streetlights on the road, and the temperature had fallen, so the roads would be slick. He would be glad when he and Kyle were safely home.

CHAPTER 8

"Wait a second," Jennifer muttered, looking around for any kind of road sign. The area didn't look like she had expected it to. On the other hand, she hadn't really expected snow during her drive.

Holding the steering wheel with one hand, she picked up her smartphone with the other to consult its map. The phone was fully charged, but the GPS didn't update to her location. That was disconcerting. "No, this is not where it's supposed to be." She traveled often, so she had the best phone on the market and the plan with the best reception nationwide. A few bars of reception flashed at the top of the screen— and disappeared as quickly as they had appeared. The message on her screen said *Out of Service Range*.

She held her phone higher and tried to cajole it. "Come on! I need reception. Come on, GPS!"

The dark asphalt of her unfamiliar path stood out against the white landscape as the snow accumulated on the surrounding dirt, grass, and trees. But the snow began falling faster than it could melt on the highway, and soon the skirling flakes left a layer of white on the road, obscuring her route. Under other conditions, she might have enjoyed the snow-covered stillness, but at the moment, she was too concerned about finding her way.

She checked her phone again, hoping for directions. Still nothing. By the time she looked up from her phone, it was too late. She was headed straight for a sharp bend in the road. With a gasp, she yanked the wheel and swerved, but missed the turn.

The coupe careened off the edge of the road and down a snowy embankment.

No! Jennifer's muscles clenched, and she held her breath. Her heart hammered. This couldn't be happening. For a moment, she could only see the pale flakes whirling past. The coupe bounced and jolted, and then the headlights showed a flash of snow-covered trees rushing up to meet the car. She cried out and held up one arm in an effort to protect herself from the collision. The world went dark.

She had no idea how long she'd been unconscious. When she became aware again, it took her several minutes to decide what to do. It was so hard to focus. She couldn't recall quite how she had gotten here. Or where "here" was. She only knew she was *in*. And she felt an urgent need to be *out*.

She pushed the door open and climbed out of the crashed vehicle in a daze. Her feet felt cold and sank into something soft beneath her, but the information barely registered. Impressions flashed through her mind: bright lights stabbing out of the darkness at her eyes, a pale world weaving strangely around her, a feeling of flight that came to an abrupt halt.

She stood still, but the landscape continued to spin around her. Black static danced across her vision. She gasped in a few breaths and tried to focus straight ahead of her: a white slope. *Upward. I need to go upward*, she thought. She wasn't quite clear on why, but she began to crawl laboriously up the hill. She felt cold and wet. She panted with the effort. *Upward*. At last, she came to a broad, flat area at the top of the slope, and she stumbled gratefully onto the level ground.

John drove the pickup truck while Kyle held the apple pie on his lap and pretended to take a bite. John kept a careful eye on the road. He was used to this kind of weather and knew better than to let down his guard.

"How's that pie?" he asked, breathing in the aroma of baked apples, cinnamon, and nutmeg.

Kyle grinned. "Still warm."

John tuned the radio to the local weather report to get an update. "…estimate has been raised to three feet in mountain areas, and we're expecting the storm to last anywhere from twenty-four to forty-eight hours," the weather forecaster said.

John chose to be as optimistic as possible in the circumstances. He glanced at his son. "Well, that sounds like good sledding weather to me."

Suddenly, a figure appeared in the middle of the road in front of the truck.

Adrenaline shot through John. He steered to one side, missing the person. Even as his heart raced, he applied slow, firm pressure on the brake pedal, and brought the truck to an expert stop. His arms were tense, his mouth open. *That was close!* His attention instantly turned to Kyle.

"You okay?" he asked.

"Yeah," Kyle answered immediately. He was uninjured, but he looked as surprised as John felt.

John replayed the last thirty seconds in his mind. What had actually happened? He had thought he was being watchful, but that person had seemed to come out of nowhere. Something must be wrong. He put the truck into park. "Hey, you stay right here, okay? Be right back." John got out of the pickup and ran toward the figure in the road. It was a woman.

"Are you okay? Are you—I'm so sorry. I didn't see you. What are you doing out here?" Even by the dim glow of his truck's taillights, he could see that the woman was beautiful and statuesque.

She gave him a curious stare. "I don't know."

Not the answer he had expected. How could the woman not know why she was out on a mountain road in a snowstorm? John rapidly switched into problem-solving mode. "What's going on? Did your car break down? Did you…are you all right?"

"I don't know."

He wondered briefly if she had been drinking. Her

speech was slurred. His medical training kicked in, and he started assessing her for symptoms of illness, intoxication, or injury.

"I don't know. I don't know." She shook her head as if trying to clear it, rubbed her eyes, then repeated, "I don't know," several more times. She wavered on her feet.

"Oh." John caught her and steadied her before she could fall. He smelled no alcohol at all on her breath, but he did notice some blood in her hair. Her confusion and dizziness could well be caused by a head injury. It seemed there was more to be concerned about than whether the woman could answer his questions. "All right, you've got quite a head laceration. We should take care of that."

He kept an arm around her as they walked to his truck. On the way, he did a rapid assessment of her state. Her eyes were open. She responded to questions, although she sounded baffled. She was walking. She lifted a hand and made a fist when he asked her to.

He opened the passenger-side door, and the interior light came on.

"Okay, Kyle. Move over, buddy." Kyle helpfully scooted toward the center and fastened himself into the middle seatbelt.

John helped the woman into the passenger seat. "Up, up, up. All the way...there we go. Watch your feet. Watch your toes." Good. She was obeying multi-step instructions. He looked at her eyes as he fastened her seatbelt. They were open, with no signs of bruising or uneven pupils that he could see. It wasn't safe to try to get to the hospital or police station in this weather. They were too far away, so he would have to take her to his house where he could perform a better examination. He shut the passenger-side door.

The woman looked at them both in confusion as John climbed back into the driver's seat. "What is *this*?"

Kyle giggled. "You just sat on a pie."

She had a bewildered expression. "A pie?"

John said, "Look, that cut on your head looks pretty bad. We should get you back and take a look at that."

The woman felt around for the cut on her head and found it.

"Gentle, gentle," John warned her.

She pulled her hand away and looked at the blood on her fingers. "Oooh."

"Ew," Kyle said, looking down and rubbing his eyes.

"It's really red," she observed in an oddly distant-sounding voice.

"Yeah," John said. She was responsive, and her words made sense, more or less. Those were good signs.

"You know what? I'm fine… I'm just going to take a little nap." She leaned over, put her head on Kyle's shoulder, and closed her eyes.

"Dad, she fell asleep on me." Kyle seemed amused and embarrassed that this total stranger had decided to use him as a pillow. "Is she gonna be okay?"

John was pleased by his son's concern for the stranger, just as Kyle had worried about the mare and the foal earlier. It showed good instincts. "I think she's going to be fine. The sooner we get her home, keep an eye on her, the better, okay?"

He glanced at the woman, only mildly worried that she'd fallen asleep. They would be home soon, and he would check her again to rule out serious injuries. Until then, they could let her rest.

"So, what are we going to do with her?" Kyle asked.

"I actually have no idea."

It was a completely new situation for John. He had encountered stray pets, wounded wild animals, and children lost in shopping malls. In all those cases, he'd made sure they made it safely back to where they belonged. But he had never come across a wounded, stray *person* before. A beautiful woman, no less. All he knew for now was that, like the animals and children he had helped, he would take good care of her.

CHAPTER 9

Light streamed through the window, waking her.
She found herself on a soft mattress, propped up
on pillows and cuddling a stuffed animal. A small dog
lying on the bed by her legs barked twice at her. She
glanced around, trying to place where she was, but the
room was unfamiliar. From beside the bed, a blond-
haired little girl holding a doll watched her.

"Hi. I'm Daisy. I'm four and a half." The girl's
smile was bright and friendly as she rattled on. "This
is my bedroom, but you can sleep in here if you want
to. Sometimes my friends sleep over. That's my dog,
Biscuit. And this is my doll, Sally. Do you have a doll?"

What a sweet, bubbly little girl.

Jennifer opened her mouth to reply, but no answer
came to mind. "I don't think so." Was she just feeling
groggy from sleep? She sat up against the pillows,
hoping the new posture would make her more alert.
Strange. It hadn't been a difficult question, so why
didn't she know the answer?

Daisy turned toward the door and yelled, "The pretty lady woke up."

Seconds later, a man came into the room. He appeared to be in his forties and tall—over six feet—with short brown hair and intense blue eyes. *Definitely handsome.* The thought surprised her. It wasn't normal for her. Or was it? Suddenly, she wasn't sure. Anyway, the man was a total stranger. Should she be worried?

"Where am I?" she asked him.

He approached the bed and spoke in a calm voice, as if afraid he might startle her. "You're okay. You're in our home. I'm John Blake, and this is my daughter, Daisy. How are you feeling?"

Her muscles ached, and her head throbbed, so this answer came more easily. "Um, kind of beat-up." She groaned, put her hands to her head, and rubbed her temples.

"Don't worry. He's a doctor," Daisy said, hugging her doll as if unconsciously trying to comfort Jennifer.

"He is?" That sounded hopeful.

"A doctor for animals," Daisy amended.

"Yes, I'm a veterinarian, but the principles are pretty much the same," her father said. "Do you mind if I take a quick look?"

Jennifer would have preferred a doctor who treated humans, but her instincts were telling her to trust this attractive animal doctor. "Sure."

"Okay. I'm just going to check out your pupils, okay?"

She glanced at the dog, who looked bright, alert, and healthy. "Yeah."

Daisy plopped herself on the bed by Jennifer's feet and watched with interest.

John pulled a penlight from his chest pocket and leaned toward Jennifer. "This might be a little bright in your eye, but I just want to see how responsive they are." He focused the beam on first one eye, then the other. She blinked and swiveled her eyes up, down, and to the sides as he went on. "Now I do have an MD coming as soon as she possibly can, but the roads are all closed from the storm."

She found it hard to digest the stream of words, but she focused on one. "Storm?"

"Yeah, there was a big storm."

Her head swam. For a split second, she had a vision of a world in black and white, then a world spinning, and then, when it stopped, a world full of color. And there was a little dog…like in *The Wizard of Oz*. What a strange thought. The man had said something about a big storm, hadn't he?

"Like a tornado?" she asked.

"No, no, like a snowstorm. Lots of snow." John let her eyes rest for a few seconds, then tested them again. "The good news is your pupils are completely responsive now, no more signs of shock. You have a mild concussion, a cut on your head, a little laceration."

Concussion? Cut? That would explain the headache. She reached up to touch the top of her head, encountered a bandage, and cried out, more from surprise than pain.

"Gentle, gentle. It's okay. It's nothing serious,

62

though. You actually seem pretty good. Do you remember anything?"

The little blonde girl reached across Jennifer and patted the dog, Biscuit, while Jennifer continued gingerly patting the bandage on her head.

"No. How did I get here?" Jennifer asked.

"My son Kyle and I, we found you wandering on the road. Do you remember that?" John gave her an expectant look, as if waiting for her to respond. When she didn't, he seemed puzzled and went on. "You got in the truck. You sat on a pie? Do you remember any of this?"

"No." Nothing he was saying rang a bell in her mind. The entire incident was a blank.

"No?"

"None of it," she insisted.

His blue eyes looked at her with such kindness. "Can you tell me your name?"

"Um, my name is, um… I'm…" As she groped through her mind for the information, it suddenly struck her. "I don't know my name." Her heart skipped a beat. "Oh my gosh, *I don't know my name*!" That was definitely not normal. The room seemed to wobble around her. Something had to be very wrong if she didn't know who she was. Her stomach looped around itself and tightened into a knot. She mentally searched for her name again. Still nothing.

"It's okay. Hey, it's okay." His tone was soothing, and the knot in her stomach began to untie itself. Someone else she knew used that tone to relax her— but she couldn't remember who it was.

John kept reassuring her. "It's really important to try and just stay calm right now. We'll work with what we do know. We'll work with the situation." His voice was so mild, so pleasant, she could keep listening for hours. For a veterinarian, he had a pretty good bedside manner.

"Let's...let's rewind," he said. "And—what is the first thing you *do* remember from before we found you? Like were you visiting someone? Were you maybe driving and got in an accident? Do you remember any of that?"

She tried to push through the fog to recall *anything* from yesterday. The fog wouldn't budge. The effort was almost painful. "I don't remember." Her vision blurred, and she wiped a tear from the corner of one eye.

"You're going to be all right—and you look good in the pajamas, which is important."

She looked down at herself and saw she was in pink pajamas sprinkled with tiny flowers. "What!" She didn't know what she had been wearing yesterday, but it hadn't been pink pj's. She was suddenly acutely aware that she was in bed, with a handsome stranger leaning close to her. "Who dressed me in this?"

He smiled as if he had expected the question. "The kids' grandmother, Bunny."

Another fair-haired girl entered the room. She was older than Daisy, wore glasses, and carried a stack of folded clothes. "And I also helped because I want to be a doctor," the girl announced. "Or a writer. Or maybe even a pilot."

"This is my older daughter, Jamie. And you know, you're going to be fine. Really," John said. Jennifer smiled and gave Jamie a faint wave. Jamie waved back as her father went on. "We borrowed some clothes for you, so when you're ready, you just put these on, you come downstairs, and we'll get you some food and fill your tummy. I'm sure that will make you feel better, okay? In the meantime, is there anything else that you need from us, anything else we can get you?"

Jennifer tried to think. Again, the question felt too hard. Discouraged, she said in a small voice, "I don't remember if I do."

He gave her a kind smile. "Okay. Well, if you do remember, you just let us know, okay? We'll be right downstairs." John and his daughters left the room, giving her some privacy.

Alone for the first time since waking up, Jennifer drew a shaky breath. How could she just forget everything like this? She would probably remember who she was soon, wouldn't she? *But what if I don't?* John and his family seemed nice enough from what she had seen, but without her memory, she was completely cut off from her life and her friends—whoever they were. What was she supposed to do now?

Maybe if she put the problem out of her mind for a few minutes, something would come back to her.

Chapter 10

Jennifer got out of bed, looked through the pile of clothes in her room, and picked out a few items, hoping they would fit. She took them with her and found the bathroom. A fresh towel and washcloth had been set out for her, along with an array of toiletries. She took a quick shower but avoided getting her bandaged head wet. After drying off, she dressed in dark jeans and a pink cotton top with a denim shirt over it. Surprisingly, everything fit her well.

By the time she got down to the kitchen, it was a beehive of activity. Daisy and a young boy in a hoodie and T-shirt sat at a large prep island in the center of the room. Jennifer assumed the boy was the son, Kyle, that John had mentioned. Strange. She remembered the boy's name, which she had just learned, but she couldn't recall her own name. A stack of pancakes and a stack of bacon occupied the center of the island, along with a pitcher of orange juice. A bowl of bananas sat to one side.

Jamie was mixing batter in a bowl while John fried an egg in a skillet.

"Careful, they're a little bit hot," John warned his kids. "Make sure Kyle gets some."

"Kyle, be careful, they're *very* hot," Jamie told her brother in an officious tone.

Holding a frying pan in one hand, John turned to greet Jennifer with a friendly, "Hey."

"Morning," Jamie added.

A nice family. Strangers, but warm, welcoming, and comforting.

Jennifer waved. The domestic scene looked pleasant and distantly familiar, like something out of a television show, with the whole family gathered, getting ready for a meal. No, not the whole family. Where was the mother? That thought made her wonder if *she* was a mother herself. Was she supposed to be in a kitchen like this, cooking for her kids? If so, was someone else taking care of them? She didn't feel like she had children, but why couldn't she remember?

"Grab a plate. Help yourself to whatever you want," John said, indicating the array of food laid out. "We've got plenty of everything. And we've got coffee, of course. How do you take your coffee?"

"Uh, I don't know." *Why does every question have to be so difficult?* Jennifer grasped at anything for an answer, and came up with, "Um, hot?"

"Hot?" John smiled at her and picked up an old-fashioned percolator coffeepot from the stove. "Good news, I've got hot coffee. Here you go." He grabbed a fresh mug and poured the steaming liquid into it. "Keep it black, and if you want any cream or sugar…"

"That's my glass," Daisy said to Jamie, who poured her some orange juice. Jennifer picked up the coffee mug.

"Do you know your name now?" Kyle asked.

Jennifer was getting used to the frustration of searching for information that simply wasn't there. "No. No, I don't know it yet. Not yet." Feeling dazed, she took a sip of coffee. "But maybe someone's looking for me?"

"Maybe you're on the news," Kyle said.

"Cable's out," Jamie informed him.

Jennifer's heart sank. "Could we see if it's posted online?"

"Internet's out, too," Jamie said with an apologetic shake of her head.

Jennifer sighed. *This keeps getting worse.* She looked down at the slippers on her feet. "Did I have any shoes?"

"You were wearing really high-heeled leather boots," John explained, "but they were soaked, and I'm afraid the heels broke. They may not be salvageable. We'll find you some better shoes."

"I know how to tie my shoes," Daisy announced to Jennifer. "Wanna see?"

"Uh, okay," Jennifer agreed absently. Daisy raised one foot wearing a boot-slipper with pompom tassels, plopped it onto the kitchen island beside her plate, and untied the bow. Surprised, Jennifer stammered, "Oh! Uh, on the counter…"

"Daisy!" Kyle scolded as his sister made a loop with one end of the string.

"On the counter, seriously?" Jamie said. She looked up at her father and observed, "At least she's wearing her slippers."

"Yeah," John said. Daisy finished the bow, and he added, "Good job, good job."

Jennifer's head spun, and she couldn't shake the feeling that she had somewhere to go or someone to find. She needed to locate *something*, and she didn't think this was the place to do it. She put a hand to her head, found the bandage, and took it off. No blood stained the gauze. She patted the top of her head to see if it hurt. Not too bad.

Daisy gave her a wide smile, as if the girl thought she was acting silly. Kyle was smiling, too.

Urgency to leave built inside Jennifer. She tried to sound nonchalant. "Okay, so my head's not bleeding anymore. That's good. Maybe I'm ready to go, 'cause I think I should find someone who knows who I am. So, I think I'm just going to go and find that human doctor, and—and thank you. But, yeah." She started toward the entryway.

Jamie looked up from the batter she was stirring and stared, wide-eyed.

"Well, the doctor's going to be here just as soon as the roads are clear. I promise," John said.

Jennifer turned to look at him but continued backing out of the room.

Jamie nodded in agreement with her father.

"Oh, no...that's okay, don't worry about me," Jennifer said. "I'll just go to the doctor. It's cool.

69

Thank you, thank you." She waved. "You're such a nice family. Bye! Thank you."

The kids exchanged confused glances.

Jennifer made a beeline for the entryway.

"There was a…there was a storm," John reminded her, but she ignored him.

Reaching the double front doors, Jennifer turned the knob on the right-hand door, but it didn't open. She jiggled the knob, turned hard, and yanked. The door swung inward—followed by a mini-avalanche. A snowdrift had left a wall of snow against the door, and quite a bit fell into the tiled entryway and onto her feet.

Jennifer gaped through the doorway at the wonderland of white before her. Everything outside was piled high with snow.

John joined her at the front door, looking out.

She turned toward him, realizing she was not at all dressed for the freezing weather. What had come over her?

"Snow?" she asked in a small voice.

"Yeah, lots of snow," he confirmed. "Lots of snow. Let's go back inside."

The kids peeked out of the kitchen to watch as their father kicked at the snowdrift until he cleared enough of the entryway that he could close the door.

Dejected, Jennifer walked back into the kitchen. She didn't know who she was, and there didn't seem to be anything she could do about it. But she did know the rumbling in her stomach was hunger, and there *was* something she could do about that. She picked up a fresh plate and helped herself to a pancake.

Chapter 11

After finishing breakfast, Jennifer followed the family into the living room. The walls were made of logs, and the room had a friendly, lodge-y feel to it. A distinctive coffee table made from polished teak-tree root commanded the center of the room. Jennifer stood by the stone fireplace. A few stockings hung from the mantel, and a pitiful, sparsely decorated Christmas tree loitered beside the wide picture window, reminding Jennifer of the poor little tree in *A Charlie Brown Christmas*. It surprised her that she could remember the cartoon but not who she was. How discouraging.

Jennifer looked around, hoping for some inspiration. "This *has* to be solvable, right? I mean you can't just get lost in the world, can you? I have to have a family somewhere, right?" The three kids, sitting on one of the sofas, nodded encouragement, and she kept talking. "Because everybody has some kind of family or friend. Like a best friend, maybe, who's looking for me?" Even as she said it, though, she had doubts. What if no one missed her? She made a small sound of despair and sat on an armchair facing John, Biscuit, the kids, and a large stuffed bear.

John said, "Of course, someone's got to be looking for you. You know what, we're all smart people here, so why don't we try to come up with what *we* can figure out about you now, okay?"

"Okay!" the kids chorused. Jennifer couldn't summon the enthusiasm to answer.

"Okay, great. So, what *do* we know about you?" John asked.

"Nothing," Kyle said.

"Kyle, not helpful. And secondly, not true," John corrected him. "Jamie, go get the chore board."

"But Dad—" Kyle started to object.

John ignored the interruption. "It *isn't* true because we know you were out on the road that night. So what were you doing out there? You were…you were out for a walk," he suggested.

"In the snow?" Jennifer asked.

From its place by the wall, Jamie got a child-sized easel with a chalkboard on one side.

"We go for walks in the snow," Daisy pointed out.

Jamie wrote "walking" on the board.

"But are you wearing four-inch heeled boots?" Jennifer asked.

Kyle answered her with a new suggestion. "Maybe you're a bank robber on the lam, and you're only pretending to have amnesia long enough to find the money you stashed in the woods."

Looking earnest and at ease, John sat on the arm of the sofa and said to Jennifer, "I'm going to guess

72

you were out for a drive. I'm going to go with that, although we didn't see a car anywhere near you that night. But either way, Jamie, *car*. Put that down."

"Okay, Dad," Jamie said, writing "car" on the chalkboard.

"Wait," Jennifer said, grasping at a ray of hope. "What about the clothes I was wearing? Because maybe in the pockets are the keys to that car or some other clue to identify me."

"I washed them," Jamie said and darted out of the room.

"Why did you wash them?" Jennifer asked.

"You sat on a pie," Daisy said, and Kyle nodded his confirmation.

Jennifer realized they had already told her this. "Oh, yeah."

Jamie came back in and handed her a shrunken sweater.

"Wait, where's the rest of it?" Jennifer asked, certain she couldn't fit into such a small piece of clothing.

"It got tiny. But I checked really carefully in all the pockets and you didn't have anything. I'm really sorry," Jamie said sadly.

Jennifer looked at the label inside the sweater and found that it was from Neiman Marcus's cashmere collection. It must have been pricey, but not designer-level expensive. How strange that she knew this but couldn't remember her own name!

"It's okay," John said. "It's all right. Let's get back to the board. We're on a roll here. We're figuring stuff out. So, you were out there..."

Jamie erased "car" and changed it to "maybe driving."

"So basically, putting it all together, you're saying that I'm here with no idea where I came from, and no idea where I was going to, and no idea if somebody is looking for me, and no idea who I am," Jennifer summarized. "But we do know that I have this one thing to my name"—she held up the sweater—"*if I had a name*." Dangerously close to dissolving into tears, she stopped talking.

"Hey." John rose, went over to Jennifer, and crouched next to her. "It's going to be okay. It really is."

His hand rested on the arm of her chair. He was so close that Jennifer couldn't help but notice his clean scent, his athletic build. His nearness was bracing. He gave off an air of quiet confidence she wished she could absorb.

"We have everything that we need here," John said. "Really, if you think about it. We've got wood for the fire to keep us warm. We have a whole cellar full of food—"

Daisy bounced to her feet and added, "And Biscuit to protect us!"

Biscuit barked, as if in agreement.

"Yeah!" Kyle and Jamie chimed in.

Jennifer was touched by how hard they were all trying to make her feel better.

"Somebody's going to come forward, okay?" John said. "I mean it. I'm going to go right now. I'm going to make some phone calls and find out if anyone is looking for you, okay?"

"Okay," she said.

John stood up and walked to the kitchen breakfast counter, saying, "You're going to be good. We're going to figure this out." He picked up the portable phone and dialed. After a moment, he said, "Is the sheriff around? Oh, still? I talked to him briefly last night, but he was stuck in Denver. He asked me to call the office today. Okay, well, I'd like to file a found-person report. No, not a missing-person report. We *found* someone last night. Anyway, we found someone without any ID and clearly suffering a little memory loss, but otherwise, she seems fine."

While John was on the phone, Jennifer gave her cashmere sweater to Jamie, hoping to make her feel a bit better about shrinking it.

Jamie thanked her and took it upstairs to put it away. When the girl returned, she was carrying two yo-yos. "We're going to do an experiment."

Jennifer was doubtful, but she was willing to try almost anything to unblock her memory. As if knowing she needed the support, Biscuit came and sat beside her in the chair.

Jamie swung a yo-yo like a pendulum in front of Jennifer, who tried to track it with her eyes.

"Follow the yo-yo back and forth," Jamie instructed her. "You are getting sleepy. Very, very sleepy."

While the yo-yo continued its rhythmic swing, Daisy stood up from the couch across from Jennifer and spread her arms. "Are you a pilot?" Daisy raised her arms overhead, touching her fingers and did a wobbly pirouette. "Are you a ballerina?" She pretended to brush her teeth with one finger. "Are you a dentist?"

Jennifer gave the same depressing answer. "I don't know." So far, this wasn't helping at all.

Daisy sat back down, looking deflated.

Jamie swung the yo-yo. "You're getting sleepy. Very sleepy."

Jennifer couldn't quite keep her eyes on the dangling toy, and frustration seeped into her.

"Are you a paleo...paleo-tologist?" Kyle asked.

Jennifer didn't answer, but her mind said, *I still don't know.*

"Are you a surfer?" Kyle ventured.

Really?

"Are you an astronaut?"

I don't know!

"You are getting very sleepy," Jamie droned.

Jennifer couldn't keep going. She grabbed the yo-yo mid-swing. "I'm getting very dizzy."

Jamie pressed her lips together in resignation and sat down next to Kyle.

Now that the kids weren't trying to play guess-the-occupation anymore, Jennifer could hear John, still talking on the phone.

"Okay, just make sure you get the word out, please. Bye." John returned to sit on the arm of the couch by the kids and hung up the phone. "All right, well, I've called just about everybody that we know and no luck yet, but they are going to get the word out," he reported, sounding upbeat. "And the sheriff and his wife—the MD—will be here tomorrow after they get back. It's going to be okay. I'm sure somebody's looking for you right now."

Jennifer petted Biscuit, feeling utterly dispirited. "Okay. I think maybe I'll go back to bed. Thank you." Her head felt like it was wearing a hat that was way too tight, and she couldn't focus her eyes. Maybe if she got some extra sleep, she would wake up feeling better. And maybe her memories would start coming back.

CHAPTER 12

Paula Marshall's office, high in a Manhattan sky-scraper, reflected her status in the entertainment industry. As hard-working as she was prominent, Paula was used to long hours. It was 8:30 pm, and she was still in her office—not an unusual thing for her. The oversized computer monitor on her desk kept her up to date on trade news while she worked.

Paula tried to make every place that belonged to her a reflection of her personal style. The walls of her office were a light blue-gray color. With an ivory leather couch, light-blue chairs, and elegant modern accents, it was the perfect place for entertaining clients, signing contracts, reviewing head shots, or relaxing with a drink. Very little hung on the office walls. An original painting graced the wall behind Paula's desk, and a large poster for *Homestyle with Jennifer Wade*, showing Jennifer's smiling face, made a statement on the wall above the table.

Paula's thoughts wandered to Jennifer and Brad. She'd hoped they might be a good fit, and that he'd help her forget the one relationship that had undermined her confidence.

Over the years, Jennifer had told Paula a great deal about her controlling ex-husband, Ashton. Jennifer had known beyond doubt that there was something very wrong with her marriage, but she'd longed for a family so much that, for three years, she'd struggled to make things work.

Their marriage had been all about how he could advance socially and professionally. He'd set her schedule and told her how to dress. Bit by bit, her self-confidence and her dreams had eroded. To make things worse, Ashton had put off having children. What Jennifer wanted had been irrelevant to him.

As a creative outlet, Jennifer had spent a lot of time cooking and decorating. Wanting to put her passion and education to good use, Jennifer had started a blog, posting essays and pictures of dishes she made. That had grown to creating entire meal plans, decorations, family activities, and even playlists of music for different types of occasions—from Valentine's Day to children's birthdays to anniversaries and graduations. Month after month, her weblog had drawn more readers, until that day eleven years ago when Paula had emailed her with a job offer. One of Paula's clients, a popular lifestyle magazine, had wanted Jennifer to write articles for them and travel around the Northeast, doing cooking and craft demonstrations.

That night when Ashton came home, Jennifer had

shared her exciting news. Instead of being happy for her, he had demanded that she turn down the job.

That had been the final straw for Jennifer. She accepted the job offer, and within a few months, she and Ashton had divorced.

Jennifer had thrown herself one hundred percent into her work, driven to prove herself. Over the course of many years writing and traveling for the lifestyle magazine, she'd built up a stellar reputation. As a result, radio and TV shows had begun asking her to do guest lifestyle spots more and more frequently. For two years, she had been a regular contributor on a cable lifestyle show. That had brought her to the attention of the Kitchen Network. Six months ago, after a flattering bidding war with two other networks, the Kitchen Network had signed Jennifer to a contract and installed her as the host of her own show.

After more than a decade of hard work, Jennifer had become an "overnight success." Yet Paula could see that Jennifer's life in New York wasn't as happy as it could be. Maybe she needed to slow down and take a short break. Paula knew it would take her friend a little while to unwind in Colorado, so she had given her a day to get settled before she called.

Paula decided to complete her last task of the day, then call. She read through a renewal contract for one of her clients who hosted a show about cats. The money was exactly the same as before, so she would have to see if she could get him a raise. She paused at the publishing section and lined out a clause about rights to books that weren't related to his show, then she popped the document in her outbox for her assistant to take care of in the morning.

Before she headed out, she grabbed her phone and dialed Jennifer's cell number. It rang and rang until voice mail picked up.

Jennifer's cheery voice said, "This is Jennifer. I can't answer my phone right now, so leave a message after the tone, and I'll talk to you soon."

It was only a recording, but Paula was glad just to hear her friend's voice. "Hello, Jennifer. I'm sure by now you have settled into the chalet and are luxuriating in your solitude. And you've probably also found the spa." She smiled and chuckled. "Listen, darling, you don't have to call me back right away. But do call me. Okay, *ciao*."

CHAPTER 13

Back upstairs in Kyle and Daisy's room, which she currently had to herself, Jennifer sat down on the bed and flopped backward, only to groan because it made her head throb. She was so disturbed by the session with John and the kids trying to help her figure out who she was that she needed to relax and not think about anything at all. She scooted herself into a more comfortable position lying on the bed and shut her eyes. When she tried to summon a memory, all she could think of was how handsome John was and how good he was with his children.

She sat up. Was there something she was overlooking? Clues to who she was that were right in front of her but she couldn't see? Probably, but then, she was having problems thinking. She folded her hands in her lap and squeezed them together. A thought struck her. She looked down at her hands, unfolded them, and held them out in front of her.

She studied her hands. There were *some* clues. She wasn't wearing any jewelry, so what did that mean?

That she had some sort of job that didn't allow her to wear jewelry? That didn't seem likely. That she was unmarried? Possibly. She looked more closely at the ring finger on her left hand. There was no tan line, no indentation to show that a ring had recently been there, so…either divorced or never married, maybe? What else did her hands tell her? She flipped them over and looked at her palms: no calluses there, so she must not do any sort of difficult physical labor like house cleaning or gardening.

She glanced at her nails. Definitely not a mechanic: there was no grease or dirt there. The nails were practical and short, with no nail polish on them, no artificial nails. There were any number of occupations that might choose to have short nails: doctors, nurses, editors, authors, typists, computer programmers, various types of musicians. Having no calluses on her fingertips probably ruled out guitarist or violinist.

On the other hand, short nails might not tell her anything at all. What if she was just a person who liked to keep her nails natural? Or what if she didn't have the money or time to get manicures? But the nails *did* look manicured—they were simply unpolished. Her hands were smooth, not chapped. Whoever she was, it looked like she groomed herself well.

Maybe other parts of her held clues. She got up, went into the bathroom, and shut the door. Pulling off the denim shirt, pink top, and jeans, she studied her reflection in the mirror as she might study someone she had never seen before. Her blonde hair was silky and was obviously cared for in a salon. Her skin was good—very few wrinkles and a clear complexion. Symmetrical features, good bone structure. The face was neither old nor young but somewhere in between. Fortyish, maybe.

Dark brown eyes. She wasn't wearing contacts, and she could both read and see long distance, so she didn't wear glasses. Good eyes then, for what it was worth, with just the tiniest hint of crow's-feet starting around them—laugh lines, she hoped.

Had she had children? Her figure was good. No wrinkles, scars, or stretch marks that she could see, either. Still, that didn't mean she wasn't a mom. Put that down as a maybe.

All in all, she would have to say she was pretty. It felt strange thinking of the woman in the mirror as pretty, when she knew that this was *her* figure, *her* face she was judging.

She turned on the faucet, let it run for a minute, and then splashed warm water on her face. She dried her face and studied it again. What was she missing?

What about all the parts of her she couldn't see: her likes and dislikes, her skills, her health, her personality? Was she a good person? Did she have plenty of friends? If so, where were they now? She heaved a sigh.

"You are a good person," she muttered to the face in the mirror. "You have *lots* of friends, maybe even a family. Tomorrow, you'll find out a lot more."

John fixed a family dinner of hot dogs and chips,

making enough to feed their visitor as well, and then sent Daisy up to get her. Kyle and Jamie sat at the breakfast bar while Jamie read *The Bobbsey Twins' Adventure in the Country*. Kyle held Biscuit on his lap.

Daisy came back into the kitchen.

"Is she coming down for dinner?" John asked.

Daisy shook her head.

"No?" He was surprised by his disappointment. He had been looking forward to more conversation with their guest, maybe even a chance to cheer her up again.

"Can I have her hot dog?" Kyle asked. He had a way of getting right to the point.

"Yeah, you sure can." John placed a second hot dog on Kyle's plate.

"What are we going to do about her?" Jamie asked.

"She's lost. We have to help her find her way home." John never could stand to see any creature suffering, much less a beautiful woman who must be feeling very afraid. He had never lost his memory, but he had lost the love of his life, and he knew how it felt to be adrift. He put some potato chips on Jamie's plate. "It's important to help those in need, including people we don't know." He smiled down at Daisy. "*Especially* at Christmas, right?"

Daisy nodded.

"As soon as we figure out who she is, she'll go back to where she's from, and then everything here will be back to normal." Even as he said it, John knew he wasn't looking forward to that day. In spite of the reason for her presence, he didn't mind their mystery visitor. In fact, he enjoyed having her here more than he wanted to admit.

He shook off the thought. He wasn't trying to replace Julie. No one could ever do that. It was natural for him to miss the kind of companionship he'd had with her, but the kids were his focus now.

"I like her," Daisy said. "She reminds me of—"

"Shh," Jamie warned.

John felt a kick in the gut at her words. Daisy looked down and didn't finish her sentence, but he knew she had meant to say their guest reminded her of their mother.

Julie had been one-of-a-kind, though. He missed her horribly, but he still had his kids, and he would always do what was best for them. They shouldn't get attached to a visitor who wouldn't be with them for long.

The sheriff and the doctor would visit tomorrow. He wondered what they might find out about her then.

At bedtime, he read the kids a story by the living room fireplace. Because their guest was upstairs, Kyle and Daisy stayed in their sleep tents in the living room. He tucked them into their sleeping bags and let Jamie go up to her room to read for another hour.

Later, after tucking Jamie in, he checked Kyle and Daisy's room out of habit. Their visitor was sound asleep, a moonbeam from the window across her lovely face.

John smiled as he quietly closed the door and headed toward his room. All was well.

86

CHAPTER 14

John woke well before dawn. He tried to go back to sleep, but found it impossible. He was aware of their mysterious houseguest in a way he hadn't experienced around a woman in a long time. He was looking forward to spending the day with her. He couldn't help but think how differently he felt about Brooke than he did about his visitor, whose very presence captured his attention.

Because of the storm, he wouldn't have any house calls to make today, but he might as well get up and shovel the front and back walkways. Sheriff and Dr. Edwards would be coming sometime today. It would be difficult for them to get into the house with a four-foot snowdrift in front of the entrance.

He fetched a snow shovel and opened the front door. Starting at waist height, he took a shovelful of snow from the top of the drift and threw it to one side. Layer by layer, he whittled the snowdrift down to ankle height. When he had a three-foot-by-three-foot area cleared, he stepped outside and closed the door behind him. Shoveling snow could be backbreaking work, but he welcomed the exercise.

When Julie was still alive, she'd often helped shovel the walkways. She didn't mind the hard work, and she always joked that it was a lot cleaner than mucking out the horse stable.

From the beginning, they had shared work, play, and dreams. They loved going horseback riding—which was almost free since Julie worked part-time at a nearby stable grooming horses a few times a week. Julie loved to laugh, and she loved music. She played guitar and wrote songs. Sometimes when John had difficulty memorizing some part of anatomy or chemistry, she would set the key concepts to music and sing him the songs to help him study. During college, John got to know her parents well: Emmett, a CPA, was a good-natured man of few words, while Bunny was a gregarious registered nurse.

It was a four-hour drive from Fort Collins back to North Creek, so John only managed to get home to visit his own parents every couple of months. During his last year of veterinary school, they'd both passed within weeks of each other—his father suddenly from an aneurysm, then his mother soon after from a broken heart. John had been devastated. Julie's family had practically adopted him then.

After completing school, John and Julie had gotten married and moved to North Creek to live in the house his parents had left him. He'd worked at a huge clinic in Boulder and commuted every day. Sometimes on the weekends, he'd taken emergency calls for Dr. Duran, the veterinarian in North Creek. Because their house had a barn, Julie had been able to fulfill a life dream to have a horse of her own. To pay for it, she'd boarded two other horses and had given riding lessons to children in the community.

After Jamie had been born, Julie's parents had taken an early retirement, and they'd moved to North Creek, where they'd found a house just up the hill from John and Julie. A few years later, Kyle had come along, and a few years after that, Daisy. But Daisy had only been one-and-a-half years old when Julie had gotten sick. A month later, Julie was gone.

At the time, Doc Duran had been leaning more and more heavily on John for help. He had been diagnosed with pulmonary fibrosis, and his doctors recommended he move to sea level. But he had been putting it off since there seemed to be no one to take over the business for him.

With Julie gone, John had decided he could no longer spend precious hours each day commuting to Boulder, so he'd offered to take on Dr. Duran's practice, and the doc had gladly agreed. In order to keep his overhead down, John hadn't rented an office. Instead, he'd invested in a good truck, made house calls, and had seen some of the smaller patients at his home office. Bunny helped with the kids and kept his medical files in order, while Emmett took care of billing and taxes.

Now John blinked and straightened and looked

around him. Absorbed in his memories of Julie, he had hardly even noticed that he'd shoveled the front walkway, the back walk, and the entire driveway. The snowplow probably wouldn't clear their street for another day yet, but the sheriff's snowmobile would have no trouble getting to the house.

Dripping with sweat in spite of the cold, he went inside and stripped off his snow clothes in the master bathroom. He showered, put on fresh clothes, and went down to cook breakfast for everyone. He didn't hear anyone moving around, and he wondered if anyone was even awake yet.

From the stack of folded clothes in her room, Jennifer chose an Irish cable-knit pullover and jeans that fit as if they had been made for her. She wondered again who the clothes belonged to. When she went downstairs, she found the kids sitting at the breakfast counter facing the kitchen where John was cooking. The gray of the sweater made his eyes look particularly blue, even from across the room.

"Good morning," Kyle said to her.

"Hi." Jennifer waved.

"Good morning," John said. He looked genuinely pleased to see her.

"Good morning," Jennifer echoed. "Hey, did anyone call for me?"

"Oh, not yet," he said. "I'm sure it'll be any minute, though. How are you feeling?"

To Jennifer's relief, she had an answer to the question. "I'm a little fuzzy still, but I'm fine."

John put a frying pan on the stove. "Okay. How about a bologna omelet?"

She blinked in surprise. *Bologna omelet?* The idea didn't exactly make her mouth water. Did those two words really belong together? Did she even like bologna? Well, she wouldn't know until she tried it. "I don't think I've ever heard of that."

Kyle cocked his head to one side and gave her a sly grin. "You've never heard of *anything*."

"Kyle!" John scolded, looking chagrined.

Jennifer wasn't upset. In fact, she enjoyed the way Kyle said what he was thinking. She gave him a sheepish smile. "No, he's right." She pointed to the breakfast John was preparing. "Can I help you?"

"Yes," he said, with more enthusiasm than she had expected.

"We'll help together," Jamie offered.

Jennifer liked the sound of that. She walked into the kitchen. "Okay, cool." She unwrapped a brown paper bundle of sliced meat. "Huh. Bologna."

"Yummy," Jamie said.

Jennifer studied the meat dubiously. "I don't think this is part of my regular diet." She rolled some meat, placed it on a cutting board, sliced it, then chopped it with quick, confident motions. That was a nice surprise. Apparently, she had decent kitchen skills.

"I've got some friends coming over that will hopefully be able to help you out," John said.

She heard him, but her attention was focused on the food prep now. "Yeah? That's cool." She wondered what she would do next. After a moment's pause, she picked up two pieces of bologna, laid one halfway across the other, sliced off a bit of the curve at the bottom, rolled them neatly together into a bologna-rose, and poked a toothpick through the base to hold it together. She handed it to Jamie. "*Voila*. A rose for a rose."

Jamie accepted it, grinning. "That's really fancy."

"I don't know how I did that," Jennifer confessed.

Raising his eyebrows, John nodded in approval of her skill.

Jamie held the bologna flower near her nose. "It smells delicious."

At the sound of a motor outside, John went to the front door and opened it. Jennifer trailed behind him to see what was making the noise. On the doorstep stood a man and a woman, taking off what looked like motorcycle helmets. Behind them on the snow was a silver snowmobile with the logo of the sheriff's office on it. The woman had short red hair, and the man was heavyset and wore a law enforcement uniform.

"Hey, good to see you." John shook hands with the sheriff. "Come on in. Hi there, it's nice to see you. It's cold out there." He turned to Jennifer. "Okay, this is Sheriff Tim Edwards and his wife *Dr.* Edwards."

"Sylvia," Dr. Edwards introduced herself, shaking Jennifer's hand.

"Hey, Tim," John said. "Our internet's been down since the storm. Is there an outage in town, too?"

"Center of town is fine," the sheriff said. "I hear it may be a few more days until the houses in your neighborhood are up and running again, though."

"We'll be fine," John said.

Sylvia took Jennifer's arm and led her to a pair of wingback chairs near the breakfast bar. "Before we start, since we don't know if you're from around here, I'll give you the usual public service announcement that I give all visitors. We're pretty high in the mountains here. Even people who are really fit can get altitude sickness—headache, dizziness, tiredness, maybe nausea. Dehydration can make it worse, so make sure you drink plenty of water."

She parked Jennifer in a chair, then sat across from her. She took out a penlight and shone it into Jennifer's right eye, then the left, studying the reaction. "Can you tell me what happened?"

Jennifer did her best to fill the doctor in. "Um, I guess I got hit on the head. But I don't remember how it happened, and I remember nothing from before that at all. The first thing I can remember is walking around in the road, and then John and Kyle found me, and then I sat on a pie." *Wait. Do I actually remember that part, or did they tell me about it?*

Sylvia continued examining her. "Hm. Any nausea or fatigue?"

"No," Jennifer said. "I mean, I'm a little bit groggy all the time, but I'm okay. And I'm hungry a lot."

"That's good." Sylvia held up her index finger and moved it back and forth. "Can you follow my finger please?" Apparently satisfied, Sylvia held her hands out, palm upward. "Okay. And press down on my arms. Good girl."

"Do you remember about where you were?" the sheriff asked.

Jennifer shook her head.

John spoke up. "We were coming back from the Barbours' place."

"It's pretty isolated out there," Sheriff Edwards said. "Do you think you might know anyone around here?"

"Gosh, I wish I did," Jennifer said. "I mean, maybe I do, I just don't remember if I do...or did."

"There's no sign of any traumatic brain injury," the doctor said.

"Really?" Then why did she still have amnesia? Jennifer was almost disappointed. If Sylvia had found an abnormality, at least there might have been a physical explanation for the memory loss.

"Motor functions and reflexes are good," Sylvia explained. Her tone was confident and encouraging. "John did a good job on the cut. Memory is a tricky thing. But you honestly seem perfectly healthy."

Jennifer absorbed this. So she no longer had any lingering signs of concussion. Nothing but wooziness and a memory full of holes. She was still deep in thought when the sheriff held something up in front of her.

"If you don't mind." The sheriff was holding a small digital camera.

Jennifer started to say, "What?"

He snapped a photo. "The deputy put out a county-wide bulletin with your description, but this picture here will really help."

The flash from the camera left bright patches in her vision. "Uh, oh okay. Great. I hope so. 'Cause I mean, there's got to be somebody out there looking for me, right?"

The back door to the kitchen opened. A couple, perhaps in their early sixties, came in dressed in heavy winter parkas.

"Hello, everybody!" the woman caroled.

"Bunny," Sheriff Edwards said.

"We came down to meet the special guest," Bunny said.

"This is Bunny and Emmett, the kids' grandparents," John said, presenting them to his houseguest.

Jennifer noticed that Bunny was several inches shorter than she was, with salt-and-pepper hair and lively blue eyes. Emmett was balding, with gray hair, a round face, and a short gray beard.

"Hi," Bunny said, moving to the front of the kitchen while taking off her gloves. "It's so lovely to meet you."

"You too," Jennifer said.

At the sound of their grandparents' voices, the kids came running and greeted them with enthusiastic hugs. Sheriff Edwards put on his parka, and Sylvia wrapped a winter scarf around her neck.

"Listen, we've got everything we need," the sheriff said. "We'll be on our way."

John shook his hand. "Thanks for coming."

Jennifer wanted to be polite and talk to Bunny and Emmett, but she still had so many questions for Sylvia.

"Take care," the sheriff said, retrieving their snowmobile helmets.

"We'll see you soon," Sylvia said.

"Absolutely," John said.

Jennifer trailed after them to the front door. "When will I start remembering things again?" she asked Sylvia.

"Two days, two weeks—you never know. But the good news is you'll eventually come out of it. I'm sure of it."

"Well, isn't there anything that I can do?" Jennifer asked. *Aren't there instructions for curing this sort of thing?*

"Good food, good sleep are really the best medicine. Call me if you need me."

"Thank you," Jennifer said, disappointed there was no pill or exercise that would make her memory return.

Sylvia left, and Jennifer closed the door after her. How disheartening. She had hoped for so much more information.

As she turned, John approached and gave her a questioning look, as if to ask, *How did it go?*

"She said I just need to eat, sleep, and relax," she told him.

John nodded, and they joined the rest of the family

in the living room. Emmett slouched in a stuffed chair near the fire. The kids were parked together on one sofa with Biscuit, and Jamie was holding a stuffed pink pig.

"Oh, sweetheart," Bunny said kindly to Jennifer, "are you starting to remember anything yet?"

"Um…" Jennifer came up with an answer more quickly than she had expected. "That I have not had a bologna omelet before." She grinned, pleased with herself. That had been humor. Wasn't that a good sign? Bologna omelet.

"Well, we can fix that," Bunny said.

"Yeah, we sure can," John agreed. He explained to Jennifer, "Bunny's also a registered nurse. I think I mentioned to you that she was the one who took a look at you the other night to make sure that you were okay. Not to mention bringing the clothes."

"Thank you. They fit really well, actually," Jennifer said.

"The clothes belonged to our younger daughter, Lisa," Bunny said. "She moved into the city and mostly wears suits. Ah, well, they're yours now." Then, as if it had just occurred to her, she asked, "Oh my goodness, what are they calling you?"

"I…I don't know. Nothing yet," Jennifer admitted.

"They get an animal in here, it's named in five minutes flat," Bunny said. "What would you like us to call you?"

Jennifer spread her arms and looked from John to

the kids for assistance. "I don't know. What do I look like?"

Daisy immediately bounced to her feet. "Sally!" she said.

"That's your doll's name, Daisy," Jamie scoffed. Daisy crossed her arms and pouted.

Bunny made some suggestions. "Carrie, Bethany, Maggie, Jenny."

Jennifer said, "Maggie? Maggie has a nice ring to it."

"You look like a Maggie," Emmett said, approving her choice.

"Oh. Thanks, I think," she said. She would start thinking of herself as Maggie. Even if it wasn't her real name, it felt like a step in the right direction. She wasn't just a nameless person found wandering on a mountain road. She wasn't a Jane Doe. This family had taken her in and given her back a name. She was Maggie now.

"Yeah, I like Maggie," John said.

Did he mean her, or just the name? Feeling a warmth creep into her cheeks, Maggie shrugged and smiled. "Yeah, me too. Cool."

"All right," John said.

Daisy made a cheering motion, as if raising pompons. "Maggie."

It was a start.

CHAPTER 15

After a breakfast of bologna omelets, Maggie washed dishes in the sink, and Bunny dried. Maggie hadn't expected to like the egg dish, but the chopped and fried-up deli bologna had proved to be a surprisingly tasty filling for the fluffy omelet. So, did liking eggs and bologna mean she could rule out being a vegetarian?

Emmett puttered around them, cleaning the counters while the kids did chores and John finished some paperwork in his basement office.

John came back into the kitchen. "Hey. So I have an idea," he said to Maggie. "What do you say we go for a ride? We get outside. We visit some people and see if anybody recognizes you."

In truth, the idea of riding around with a man she barely knew—even one she trusted—was a bit intimidating for Maggie. *What will I say? What if we have nothing to discuss? Or what if I make a fool of myself? What if we disagree about life or politics?* On the other hand, she found the idea of spending more time in his company exciting. She had to admit she found him appealing. She decided she didn't mind the prospect of being alone with him.

"Sounds like a good idea," Maggie said.

"Bunny, you okay watching the kids for a while?" John asked.

"Oh, get out of here," Bunny urged. "Enjoy yourself. There's nowhere prettier in the world."

"Come on." John said to Maggie. On their way out of the kitchen, he put a hand on Bunny's shoulder. "Thank you."

John found Maggie some appropriate clothes, and they bundled up for outdoor activities. They wore gloves, snow pants, and hooded parkas trimmed with faux fur. Outside the front door, he put on a helmet with a visor and gave one to Maggie.

She put it on carefully, worried that it might hurt the top of her head, but her head only felt a little sore, and the inside of the helmet was well padded. So far, so good.

Now the bright red snowmobile in front of them was another thing. It looked fast and powerful. There were no seatbelts.

"I'm not getting on that thing," she announced.

"Oh yeah, you are," John said, climbing onto the vehicle and starting the engine. He wasn't so much telling her what to do, as encouraging her, inviting her. "Come on, hop on."

She hesitated. "Where are we going?"

"Just around the neighborhood."

That didn't sound too scary. One little ride would be fine. She climbed onto the snowmobile behind him.

Maggie felt strangely shy. She liked what she knew of John so far, but hugging him? Pressing against him? That seemed a bit overfriendly. She swallowed hard and looped her arms gingerly around him.

"Hold on tight," he advised in a light tone, setting the vehicle in motion.

They were going so fast! As the snowmobile zoomed forward, Maggie nervously tightened her grip and leaned against John, which she found surprisingly comforting. John pointed out his neighbors' houses, and Bunny and Emmett's house up the hill. The scenery was amazing—snow-covered mountains and trees in every direction. After a while, her fear began to melt away.

Had she spent much time outdoors in the snow? She doubted it. It was a strange sensation.

The world looked new and magical, all draped in white. As they rode across the snowy ground, it reminded Maggie of the song "Jingle Bells." A light spray of powder snow sprinkled her face. She was enjoying herself so much she relaxed a bit. John sped up and did a few zigzags. He was a good driver, and she felt safe. *Dashing through the snow...* This was the real thing—amazingly fun. She was certain now she had never done anything like this.

"This is your neighborhood?" she yelled above the noise of the snowmobile's engine.

He zigged and zagged again.

She finally threw her arms over her head, laughing. "Woohoo! Wow!" When she put her arms around John again, it wasn't out of fear.

O'er the fields we go, laughing all the way. What a wonderful song. They drove and drove, and Maggie didn't feel the slightest bit cold.

John pulled the snowmobile up in front of a house decorated with multicolored Christmas lights. He dismounted and helped Maggie off the vehicle. They went to the front door and knocked.

A man with a short brown beard opened the door. "John! Good to see you."

"Good to see you," John replied, shaking his hand.

"Hi," Maggie said as they entered the house.

John introduced Maggie to Stan and Holly Barbour. The man looked about John's age, and the woman, maybe five years younger. Holly had light brown hair and wore a flour-dusted green Christmas apron that looked as if kids had made it. The apron gave Maggie a mental image of mother and children working together using scissors and fabric and happy imaginations. There was a sweetness about that image that rendered the apron charming, as far as she was concerned. And the green color looked cute on Holly.

"We have been snowed in the last few days with the kids, so," Stan said, leading them through the dining room, "we decided to make the best of it and really do up the tree this year." He showed them to the living room, where a Christmas tree loaded with ornaments stood in the corner just past the fireplace.

"Oh wow. Nice," John said.

Stan introduced Maggie to the group of children—six of them—all of whom were working on Christmas decorations.

"Here," Holly said, handing a glass punch cup full of creamy liquid to Maggie. "I just made eggnog."

"Eggnog," Maggie said, accepting the cup. "Oh." She took a sip. It was sweet and thick, with notes of vanilla, cinnamon, and nutmeg. Almost like drinking a custard milkshake, she decided. "Wonderful."

"Family recipe. Someday it'll get me on TV and make me rich," Holly said with a chuckle.

Something about the idea of making eggnog on TV tickled at the back of Maggie's brain. Maybe she enjoyed watching TV shows about cooking? Yes, that sounded right. That might even be where Maggie had gotten the idea to make a rose out of bologna.

"And you arrived just in time," Stan said, crossing to the Christmas tree. "We're about to put up the star. This is their favorite part. You ready?" he asked one of his daughters. "Where's your star? One, two, three," he said as he hoisted her up and she placed the star on the top of the tree.

Maggie saw John's face brighten as he gazed at the decorated tree. The two of them exchanged a look. There was an air of love and connectedness in this room, a special sense of *family* that radiated to everyone. Maggie and John shared that moment, letting the feeling wash over them as their gazes met and held.

"Now it feels like Christmas," Holly said, clasping her hands in front of her.

It really did feel like Christmas, Maggie realized. She wondered again if she had a family and if they were out looking for her. The very idea seemed unreal right now. Yet, here she was with total strangers, surrounded by a warm, loving feeling. This was what the holidays were really about. More than anything else—even more than getting her memory back—*this* was what Maggie wanted for Christmas.

"You have a beautiful home," Maggie told Stan and Holly. "I'm sorry to intrude on your family time at the holidays."

"You're not intruding," Stan said. "John and I have been friends since high school. He's like family."

"I appreciate that, Stan," John said. "But Maggie's right. We should get out of your hair. We mainly stopped by to see if anything here jogged Maggie's memory."

"What do you mean?" Holly asked.

"I...I don't know who I am." Maggie cringed, though she knew she had no reason to be embarrassed. Her memory loss wasn't her fault. At least, she didn't think it was. "Maggie probably isn't my real name. John found me on the road near here during the snowstorm, so I was hoping I'd see something in this area that seemed familiar, or that maybe you knew me."

"Oh, I'm so sorry." Holly touched Maggie's arm. "And at the holidays. You poor thing."

"You haven't seen her before?" John asked. "Or maybe seen a car off the road? She has a head laceration, so we think maybe she was in a car accident."

"No," Stan said. "I wish we could help."

"We'll be on the lookout for a car," Holly said.

"Thank you," Maggie said, suddenly tired. Her head buzzed, and her knees felt wobbly. She grabbed John's arm for support.

"Whoa, there," John said, steadying her. "I think this is enough excitement for one day. Let me get you back home." He steered her to the front of the house, and she was grateful for the help.

Holly opened the door for them. "Are you okay to ride on that snowmobile? You could stay here and rest."

"No, thank you. I'll be fine," Maggie said. All she wanted was to get back to Biscuit and the kids and the warm fire and cozy couch. To get *home*. Funny that the word had come to mind, even though she knew the home wasn't hers.

"I'll make sure she's okay on the way back," John said. "Merry Christmas to you all."

"Merry Christmas," Stan said.

"Let us know if you need anything," Holly called, waving.

"We will," John said, walking Maggie to the snowmobile as Holly shut the door. "You sure you're up for this?" he asked.

"Yes, just take me home."

John grinned. "You got it." He held her hand as she

climbed on behind him, then guided her arm around his waist. "Hold on."

Maggie put her other arm around him. She didn't mind being so close to him. He was handsome and strong. And caring. And he smelled like spicy aftershave and the outdoors.

He started the snowmobile and put it into gear. As it lurched forward, she held tighter.

"You okay?" he asked.

"Yes." *More than okay.* Should she feel guilty? *What if I have a boyfriend waiting for me somewhere?* Not knowing bothered her. She wanted to be free to enjoy this moment, but...

Her eyes prickled with tears. In a flash, she'd gone from a perfect holiday afternoon to being troubled and anxious.

"It's going to be okay, Maggie," John said, as if reading her mind. He patted her arm. "We'll figure this out. I promise."

Somehow, when he said it, she could believe it. She relaxed against him as they sped across the snow toward home.

CHAPTER 16

After a nap with Biscuit in Kyle and Daisy's room, the buzzing in Maggie's head subsided, and she felt much better. A delicious aroma wafted up the stairs. She could almost place what it was, but not quite. She headed down to see what was cooking.

The sun was down, so the lamps were on and the fire was lit, giving the place a warm glow. John was stirring a pot on the stove while Jamie folded napkins and Daisy and Kyle colored at the breakfast bar. A cozy scene that put her at ease. Maggie inhaled the fragrant air—savory beef with onions and spices—and knew immediately what it was.

"Mmm, stroganoff," Maggie said. *Comfort food.*

John turned to her. "You *know* stroganoff?"

Pleasantly surprised with herself, she met his blue gaze. "I do. Yes!"

"The mind is an amazing thing," he observed, giving her a warm smile.

Her heart skipped a beat at the sight of his smile. Unbidden, an image popped into her mind: riding with John on the snowmobile, pressed against him, her arms around his waist. Such a wonderful feeling. Embarrassed at the train of her thoughts, she looked away with a self-conscious laugh.

There was a knock on the back door, and without waiting for it to be answered, a white-bearded man in a ski cap entered, just as Emmett and Bunny had earlier in the day.

"Smells good," the man said.

The kids called out a greeting.

"Hey, Dan," John said as the man took off his jacket. "Dan, this is Maggie. Maggie, this is Dan."

They exchanged hellos. The newcomer seemed relaxed and casual, as if this were a second home to him. From what Maggie had seen, the Blake household in general seemed to be an open, welcoming place.

"You want a bowl?" Jamie asked the new arrival.

"Don't go to any fuss for me," Dan said, pulling off his cap to reveal fluffy gray hair on a slightly balding head.

Apparently Dan ate here often. Maggie looked around, wondering where they could all sit. Something inside her yearned to gather this group at one table and eat together. Like a family. Her eyes settled on the long dining table that was piled with books, toys, and papers. "Ooh, hey, can I set the table?" she asked. "I'd really like to."

"Um, well…" John said.

"We never set the table," Jamie explained with a shrug that made her long blonde pigtails jiggle. She looked at her father and made a decision. "But let's do that."

Pleased that Jamie had liked her suggestion, Maggie headed for the table and cleared away the accumulated mess.

"Pull up a chair, Dan," John said. "It looks like we're having a formal dinner tonight."

"Formal? I didn't know you knew what that was," Dan teased. To Maggie, he said, "So you must be some kind of Martha Stewart or something."

Martha Stewart. "I know who that is!" Maggie said. There were definitely things she remembered. Unfortunately, none of them had shed any light on who she was. She got out six stoneware plates with denim blue rims and set them on the table. From another cupboard, she got clear pint glasses. "Do you have any candle holders?"

John said, "There are some crystal ones in the china cabinet."

"But we haven't used those since—" Jamie stopped abruptly.

Maggie noticed the distress on her face. "That's fine. We don't have to. It's not important."

"No, it's okay," Jamie said. "We should use them."

"Then that's what we'll do," John said. When he looked at Jamie, Maggie thought she saw a hint of pride at his daughter's mature decision.

Maggie gave Jamie and John a grateful smile. It was so kind of them to offer to use the candlesticks, even though they might bring some sad memories.

When the table was set, John said, "Would you look at this? It's gorgeous."

"Maybe you're a professional table setter," Jamie suggested in all seriousness.

Maggie found the compliments heartening and the idea of being a table setter amusing.

John brought a steaming pot to the table. "Seriously. You do seem to have a knack for decorating."

"Well, my 'knack' wants me to put this in a serving bowl." Grinning, Maggie took the pot and pointed John toward a chair. "I can take care of it."

"You two wash your hands," Jamie told her brother and sister.

Daisy hopped down from her barstool and headed for the sink. Kyle made a face, but he followed.

Maggie scooped the stroganoff into a large bowl she found and brought it to the table. "There. Much better. Though I guess I'll have to settle for putting the salad dressing bottle on the table. I didn't see any cruets."

"Never mind. It's perfect," John said. "Let's eat."

Dan peered into the serving bowl. "Don't tell me—beef stroganoff?"

Maggie saw a look pass between Dan and John, but wasn't sure what it meant. "I like stroganoff," she said. "At least, I'm pretty sure I do."

"Me, too," Dan said. "Just not every night."

"Dad makes it a lot," Jamie told Maggie. "So does Grandma."

Maggie wondered if they made stroganoff so often

because it reminded them of Julie or because it was a hot meal that could be prepared quickly for a family. Maybe it had simply become habit.

"A little variety wouldn't kill you," Dan grumbled, jabbing at a cluster of noodles.

Maggie wondered why Dan didn't make his own food if he didn't like what John made. She could see that Dan's "complaints" were more teasing than serious, however.

"I don't know what variety is," Daisy said. "But I'm pretty sure it tastes yucky. I *like* what Daddy makes."

Maggie hid a smile at the little girl's staunch defense of her father.

"You're right," Dan said with his mouth full. "This is delicious. And I got no right to complain, seeing as you're feeding me."

"Do you cook, Dan?" Maggie asked, trying not to imply criticism of John's curmudgeonly friend.

"Nah. Not if I can help it. Don't feel much like it after snowshoeing or skiing all day."

"Dan spends a lot of time in the back country getting inspired," John explained. "Speaking of which, keep an eye out for a car stuck in a snow bank. We think Maggie might have been in a car accident."

It was nice of John to ask his friend to help, although Maggie doubted Dan would pick up any helpful clues while rambling around on snowshoes.

"It might have been a plane crash," Kyle suggested.

Jamie shook her head and looked despairingly at

him through her glasses. "Not a plane crash. Maggie would have been hurt a lot worse if it were."

"A flying saucer, then," Kyle proposed.

Jamie seemed to have the makings of a serious scientist, while Kyle seemed more suited to be a fiction writer. Or maybe they were like those two FBI agents on TV who looked into alien sightings. Maggie couldn't remember the name of the show. Of course.

"Let's stick with the car theory for now," John said.

"Sure," Dan said, with his mouth full. "I'll keep an eye out."

"Can we play games after dinner, Daddy?" Daisy pleaded.

"Okay," John said. "Or...we can read Christmas stories. It's up to you guys."

"Stories!" the kids cried in unison.

"Which ones should we read?" John asked.

"Do you have a lot of Christmas books?" Maggie asked, placing her fork and napkin on her empty plate.

"Not many," Kyle said. "Only two shelves."

"Two *bookshelves* full?" Maggie asked, impressed.

"We like books," Jamie said. "But we all like different ones, so it's hard to choose, and sometimes we argue."

"Nonsense," Dan said. "No arguing allowed at Christmas. I'll help you sort it out."

"Okay!" Kyle dropped his fork, pushed back his chair, and leapt to his feet in one motion.

Daisy scooted down from her chair.

"Wait!" Jamie said. She turned to their father and primly asked, "May we be excused, please?"

Daisy giggled and Dan snorted. Kyle looked confused. But John seemed to catch on.

"Why yes, dear daughter," he intoned formally. "You may be excused, provided you three children wash your faces and hands, brush your teeth, and put on your night clothes."

"Night clothes?" Kyle said. "Why are you talking funny?"

"Come on," Jamie said, pulling him away. "We don't have to do dishes!"

The children scampered off.

"Sir Daniel," John said with a courtly air, "you may be excused, as well."

Dan rolled his eyes and headed for the stairs.

John gathered the plates and scraped the uneaten food into the garbage. "They didn't exactly lick their plates clean. I guess it wouldn't hurt to branch out more often."

"Maybe I could give it a try." Maggie thought she knew how to cook. She felt like she might, and she had shown decent knife skills when dicing bologna.

"That would be nice. I'd appreciate that." He held her gaze, a slight grin on his face.

Maggie forgot to breathe for a second. She was pretty sure he had the bluest eyes she'd ever seen, and she could swear they were twinkling. *Do eyes actually twinkle in real life?* She shook her head to clear her thoughts. "So," she said, trying to turn the subject to something that wouldn't make her want to keep gazing into his eyes. "That friend of yours, Dan. He's like a… mountain man?"

"Yeah." John chuckled. "He kind of is. But he's also a pretty famous painter, a fine artist."

"Really?"

"Yeah. Dan Daniels is his name. He moved out here years ago. I actually have a book of his."

John got the book and laid it on the breakfast bar. Maggie sat on one of the high barstools while he stood with one arm around the back of her chair, leaning in so that they could look at the art together while she leafed through the pages. She was acutely aware of his closeness, the smell of his soap, his arm almost around her, his hand only inches from hers…

She quickly pulled her mind back to the artwork and flipped a page.

"I like this one," Maggie said, pointing to a painting of bamboo in the coffee table–sized hardcover. She turned a few more pages, then stopped. A little zing of realization ran up her spine. "I've seen this one before."

John's brows shot up. "You have? Are you sure?"

"Yeah. I've definitely seen it. Is it in an art museum or something like that?"

John read the description next to the picture. "It's called 'Bridge Over Blue River,' but it doesn't say where it is. But I can ask him. I mean, maybe it will tell us where you're from."

"Maybe," she said. "Anything's worth a try." She

stared at the image of the painting for a long time, relishing the feeling of recognition.

Did she have a family of her own? Or friends, at least?

What if Dan held a clue about who she was? That would be amazing. Or would it? If she learned who she was, it would probably mean an end to her time here. She wanted to get her memories back, but she was afraid to lose this new feeling of belonging that she had found with John and his kids.

CHAPTER 17

Maggie went to the sink and filled it with soapy water while John collected more dishes. She couldn't help being excited about finally finding a clue about herself. But what if she was a terrible person that no one liked? What if she talked in movie theaters and tailgated and hated puppies and kittens? She didn't *feel* like that type of person. She liked dogs—well, Biscuit, anyway. Biscuit seemed to like her, too, which meant she couldn't be too bad of a person, right?

"Earth to Maggie," John said.

"Huh?" Maggie hadn't heard him come back into the room. She turned from the bowl she was washing.

"I was trying to tell you that you don't need to hand wash that. It's fine to run it through the dishwasher."

"But Bunny wanted everything washed by hand, so I thought—"

He grinned. "That's just Bunny. She's old-fashioned that way. We load it all—crystal, china, everything. In the big picture, what's a couple of water spots or a scratch? Throwing it all in the dishwasher gives me more time with the kids."

"I like the way you think." She loaded the bowl in the dishwasher, along with the plates and glasses, while John wiped the table.

As they were finishing up, a giggling commotion arrived in the kitchen: the three kids and Dan with a stack of books.

"Hey, I thought you were helping them narrow down which book to read," John said.

"No, I said I'd keep them from arguing," Dan said with a smirk.

"We didn't argue!" Daisy said. "Do we get all the stories?"

"We'll see," John said. "You kids head into the living room and get settled. I'll be there in a minute."

"Maggie, too?" Daisy asked.

"I hope so." John looked at Maggie.

There was that smile again. She wanted to spend more time with him, and it felt good to think he wanted her there, too. "I wouldn't miss it." She turned back to the sink and fiddled with the sponge so he couldn't see her blush.

"Yay!" Daisy ran to the living room with her siblings close behind.

"I'll be off, then," Dan said.

"Wait," John said. "We might have a lead on Maggie's identity, and I think you can help."

"I don't know what I can do, but I'm happy to try."

"I was showing her your paintings, and she recognized one."

"Really? Which one?" Dan joined John at the breakfast bar where the book lay open. "Oh, this one was sold years ago."

"Where? Do you have records of who bought it?" Maggie didn't want to get her hopes up, but this was the first real lead they'd had.

"It was part of a show I did in a gallery...East Coast someplace, but I don't remember the city. If I can figure out which gallery, they might have records of who bought it."

"Would you mind, Dan? It may be a long shot, but it would mean a lot to have a place to start," John said.

"Of course," Dan said. "But don't hold your breath. It's the holidays. I suspect I won't be able to get hold of anyone until the new year."

Maggie realized she had literally been holding her breath, and she let it out. She hoped she wouldn't still be waiting for an answer by New Year's. If no one came looking for her before then, what kind of life could she possibly have to go back to? A life where no one missed her during the holidays? A life without friends or family or love?

"I understand," she said. "Thank you." A new thought occurred to her—a terrible thought. What if the Blakes didn't want her here in their house, and they were just being kind? She had thrown them out of their normal routine. The kids were sleeping in the living room. She was eating their food. What if she was imposing, and they were just too polite to say so? She needed to find out.

"Yeah, thanks, buddy," John said, walking him to the back door. "Careful out there." He closed the door behind Dan and turned to Maggie.

She took a deep breath. "John, I've been thinking," she said haltingly. "Maybe I should move into a hotel in town now?" She felt hot and cold all at once. She had actually suggested leaving. Out loud. *Please, please say no!*

He hesitated, as if trying to find the right words. "Well, sure, that might be possible. Except we're a resort town here, and it's ski season. Even if they have a room available, it'll be expensive. They'll ask for ID, an upfront payment, and a credit card to charge for the rest."

Maggie blanched. What had she been thinking? She didn't even know who she was, much less have ID. What if real-life Maggie couldn't afford an expensive resort? She couldn't just blithely ask John to pay for it. "Oh, I'm sorry! It's just that I don't want to intrude on your family, especially during the holidays."

"I want to do what's best for you," John said earnestly. "If you ask me to, I'll set up a hotel. But staying with us is no problem at all."

Yes! a voice inside her sang. But she couldn't leave it at that, just because it was the answer she wanted to hear from him. "Are you sure that—"

"It's not a bad feeling," John said. "Having you with us, I mean."

Gratitude flowed through her. She didn't want to be alone in the world. "You've been so generous, and your home is the only home I know right now."

"Maggie—" he began.

"It's not a bad feeling," she said, echoing his words. They smiled at each other, and she found herself getting swept away in the ocean of his blue eyes again.

"Maggie, it's Christmas. You can't be alone."

She was glad he wanted her to stay. So glad and grateful. Her suggestion of leaving had been based on the fear that she was imposing and that he might secretly resent her. She hadn't even stopped to think it out. "Maybe just another day or two. But I want to do my part to help around here. Now, isn't it story time?"

At the end of the evening, John read the final bedtime story aloud in front of a fire in the living room fireplace. Maggie and the kids sat across from him, crowded together on one sofa, a cozy audience listening with rapt attention.

This last book was a family tradition during the holidays. He and Julie had started the custom before Jamie had taken her first step. How precious his memories were of Julie reading to him and the kids. "This is where the magic happens," she had told him with each tradition they'd created.

John glanced at Maggie. She was good with the kids, and they were drawn to her. In fact, she was so good with them that he knew she *must* have a family waiting for her, missing her. She was creative and beautiful and caring. How could she *not* have a husband or fiancé or at least a boyfriend worrying himself sick about her? The answer was obvious: she did.

John understood all too well the pain of losing someone so dear to him. He could never wish that kind of torment on anyone else. He believed it was his obligation to relieve suffering wherever he found it. These were values he worked every day to teach his children. That's why he was honor bound to find Maggie's family and restore her to them, just as he would have wanted a Good Samaritan to bring Julie home if she had been lost. It was his duty to *prevent* suffering, too, if he could. He couldn't let himself or the kids get so attached to Maggie that they would be hurt when she had to leave them. Julie had been his one great love. He had his memories of her, and he had Jamie, Kyle, and Daisy. That would have to be enough.

As John read the lyrical story, he found comfort in the tradition of love it represented. Its healing warmth reached deep inside him. There was a feeling of bittersweetness when he reached the end and had to read the final line. "And when the presents were all unwrapped and Christmas Day was done, a single star shone in the sky, and its light warmed up the whole world."

He looked up to find that Maggie had fallen asleep on the couch with the children snuggled around her like drowsing puppies.

The sight melted his heart.

CHAPTER 18

"Maggie!" Daisy exclaimed the next morning, running to meet her at the bottom of the stairs.

"Good morning," Maggie said as Daisy hugged her. The little girl's personality was so sweet and open that Maggie was already fond of her and automatically returned the hug. "What's that awesome smell?" she asked, though she was pretty sure she recognized the aroma from her first morning there.

"My favorite—pancakes," Daisy announced.

"And coffee," John called out. "Hot, just like you like it."

Daisy pulled Maggie into the kitchen, where Jamie was flipping pancakes at the stove, wearing a red apron almost as big as she was. Maggie lifted Daisy up and deposited her on a stool at the breakfast bar next to Kyle. She crossed to the coffeepot to pour a cup, but John had beaten her to it. As she accepted the steaming mug from him, their fingers touched—an almost electrical sensation—and she returned his smile. Was his smile warmer this morning, or was she imagining it? "Thank you."

"How'd you sleep?" John asked.

He didn't sound like he was just being polite. It seemed like he really wanted to know. "A bit restless. Lots of dreams," she answered.

"Oh? Did they help you remember anything?"

"Not exactly." She sipped the black coffee and decided to add some cream. "I'm sure I was dreaming about my past, but when I woke up, it vanished. I can't remember a thing. It's like finding out all over again that I don't know who I am."

"Well, don't try to force it. Trust your instincts, and I think things will start to come back." He went to the doorway and turned. "Maggie?"

She stopped fussing with her coffee and looked at him. "Yes?"

"Would you like to go into town with me later? I have to check on a patient, and I thought we could walk around a bit. You know, to see if anything helps jog your memory."

"I'd like that."

"Then it's a date! I mean, a plan. You know." He shoved his hands awkwardly into the pockets of his jeans.

She smiled. "I knew what you meant." Even so, her stomach fluttered as if a hundred butterflies had taken flight inside her.

He smiled back. "I'll phone Bunny and see if she'll watch the kids."

"They won't be coming with us?" Maggie would have enjoyed taking the kids, but at the same time, the thought of an afternoon alone with John sent the butterflies fluttering again.

"I thought we could do some window shopping for Christmas. That is, if you don't mind helping."

"I don't mind at all. Sounds like fun."

"Good, good. I'll ask Bunny to come down after lunch."

"Then it's a *plan*," she said, emphasizing "plan" so he knew she knew it wasn't a date. She thought she saw a tinge of pink on his cheeks before he turned and went through the door.

After lunch, with the kids and Bunny clustered around a jigsaw puzzle, John and Maggie climbed into the truck. Maggie noticed an old-fashioned black doctor's bag.

"Do you keep your veterinary supplies in here?" she asked.

He glanced at it. "Yeah. My dad gave it to me."

It was the first time he'd mentioned his own family, and she was curious to know more. "Was he a vet, too?"

John put the truck in gear and headed down the driveway. "He was a surgeon in Denver, actually, but he semiretired to be a country doc here in North Creek after I came along. I was a bit of a surprise—my parents were older and had already resigned themselves to not being able to have kids when they found out mom was pregnant with me."

"Then you're an only child?"

"Yup, but they made sure I had lots of other kids to play with. That's one of the reasons they moved here. To give me a wholesome, small-town upbringing."

Maggie wished she had something to tell him about her own past, to contribute to the conversation, but she realized she had no idea if she was a country mouse or a city mouse. Was she an only child? Were her parents still living? If so, were they looking for her?

After a short drive, he pulled the truck to the curb in front of a small house. "We're here."

"Should I wait in the truck?" Maggie asked, not sure what would be appropriate.

"Absolutely not. Nancy and Katy will enjoy meeting you. Come on."

The door was answered by a grandmotherly woman with glasses and short, graying hair. "Won't you come in? I've made some tea, the kind John likes. Some cookies, too."

"How's our little patient doing?" John asked as they followed Nancy inside.

"So much better." Nancy led them to the kitchen.

"It smells wonderful in here," Maggie said.

"I just baked gingersnaps—my secret recipe."

John squatted down beside a fluffy, cream-colored cat with a dark brown face. "Hi, sweetie. How are you feeling?"

"Oh, she's beautiful," Maggie said.

After examining the cat, John said, "Katy's really healing well, Nancy. The swelling in her leg has gone down, and she doesn't flinch when I touch it. But try to keep her quiet until Christmas. Then you can give her a new toy."

Nancy's face lit up at John's good report. "That's perfect timing. I already bought Katy a pink feather for her stocking."

"I'm sure she'll love it," John said. "In the meantime, I'm just a call away if you have any concerns."

How caring he was, both with the cat and her owner. Drawn to the kindness in his face and voice, Maggie found it hard not to stare at him.

Nancy patted her shoulder. "John told me about your memory loss. In my experience, a good, hot cup of tea always sets my mind right. Please, have a seat."

John and Maggie sat at the table.

Nancy set a china teapot in the center of the table and then carefully rotated it a few degrees. "You know, in some cultures, it's considered rude to point the teapot at someone."

"I had no idea," Maggie said. "At least, I don't think so."

At Nancy's request, John poured the tea.

"Now, Maggie," Nancy said. "Try the tea and see what you think. Then we can add milk and maybe a lump of sugar, if it suits you. Your taste buds will remember what they like, even if you don't."

"That's a good way of looking at it." Maggie brought the dainty cup to her lips and tasted the warm and aromatic liquid. Slightly bitter, but still pleasant. "I know this flavor. It reminds me of… I want to say Earl Grey. But that's not quite right. There's something else in there."

"It does have the bergamot oil that's in Earl Grey. But you're right—there is something else." Nancy stirred some milk into her own cup. "I think milk enhances the flavor. See what you think." She poured some into Maggie's cup.

Maggie inhaled deeply as she watched the milk swirl into the tea. The scent was…floral. It was…she picked up the cup and sipped, and this time she knew immediately. "Lavender! Am I right?"

John laughed. "How did you do that?"

"The milk really brought out the essence," Maggie said.

"You have a discerning palate, young lady. But let's see if you can figure out the secret ingredient in my gingersnaps." Nancy held out a plate of cookies, and they each took one.

John ate his in three bites, "mm-ing" under his breath. He took a second cookie.

Maggie chewed slowly, letting the flavors cascade over her palate. The names of the ingredients popped into her head. "Cinnamon. Cloves. Ginger, of course. Molasses, honey, and brown sugar. And butter. A bit of whole wheat flour, as well as all-purpose. Is that right?"

Nancy nodded.

"Wow," John said. "You got all that?"

Maggie was almost as surprised as John. Did these tiny drips of memory mean the dam would soon break? If so, what if she didn't *want* it to? What if her life before North Creek didn't give her the feelings she was starting to have here with John and his children? What if those feelings had been missing from her life until now?

"But what's the secret ingredient?" Nancy said. "No one has ever guessed it before."

Secret ingredient... Maggie sipped some tea to clear her palate, took another bite of cookie, closed her eyes, and savored. "I think *maybe...*" Maggie opened her eyes. "Will you tell me if I'm right?"

"Only if you both swear not to tell."

"Of course," Maggie said. "Is it a hint of... cayenne?"

Nancy's mouth dropped open. "Yes—that's it!"

"I'm impressed," John said. "I had no idea." He took another cookie.

"I think Katy's impressed, too," Maggie said, laughing. The cat had climbed onto her lap and made herself comfortable. Maggie stroked the unbelievably soft fur.

"She doesn't let just anyone do that," Nancy said. "Do you have any pets of your own?"

Maggie's breath left her in a rush as she struggled to think. "I...I don't know! What if I do? I love animals, so I might have one." She gulped.

"I'm so sorry, I completely forgot," Nancy said.

Horrified, Maggie said, "My dog or cat could

be all alone, starving and terrified!" She stood up, gently placed the still purring Katy on her chair, and began pacing. She *needed* to do something, but didn't know what. The more she thought about it, the more agitated she got.

John went to Maggie and put his hand on her shoulder. "I know I've only known you a few days, but I can tell you're thoughtful and caring." His voice was soothing. "You'd never have left home without arranging for someone to look after your pets."

"Really?" She wanted to believe him.

He put a finger under her chin and tilted her face up so she could look at him. "Really." His blue eyes crinkled with gentle humor as he added, "Trust me. I'm a doctor. I know what I'm talking about."

Maggie couldn't help laughing with relief. "Okay, Doctor. I'm sorry I panicked a bit."

"What's afternoon tea without a little panic?" John said. "But we'd better get started on our Christmas shopping now."

Before they left, Nancy handed John two parcels. "A little Christmas gift: *Morning in Paris*—the tea you like—and cookies for your darling kids. But don't give away my secret ingredient."

They hugged Nancy and thanked her. "Your secret's safe with us," Maggie assured her.

CHAPTER 19

John took Maggie to downtown North Creek. When they got out of his truck, the first thing Maggie noticed was a community bulletin board plastered with "Found" flyers displaying the sheriff's photograph of her and asking for tips from anyone who might have information about her. They both paused to study a flyer.

"Oh," Maggie said. She didn't object to seeing her face so prominently displayed. For some reason, that didn't feel strange at all. But that embarrassing shot with her mouth open? She grimaced. "That's not a very flattering picture."

"You do look a little surprised," John agreed, "but it gets the job done." They strolled together past several shops.

A window display caught Maggie's eye, and she stopped to look. In the display, a pair of red mittens lay on a small table. Each mitten had a single white snowflake design and lace ribbon trim at the cuff. An image of an almost identical set of mittens—though much smaller—flashed through her mind with a *zing* of recognition.

"Oh my gosh," she said. "I think I had a pair of mittens just like that when I was a kid. Is it possible I could remember something from that far back?"

John shrugged. "I don't think there's any rules to how this all works. But, I mean, was it a good memory?"

He's right. I feel happy. I should focus on that. Maggie gazed at the mittens again. This time, the mental image was stronger. "Yes. I think I asked my mom for a pretty pair of mittens, and she made them for me—with all the snowflakes and the beads and even the ribbons." She turned from the window, filled with emotion, and he was right there in front of her. "Yeah, it's a really happy memory."

It felt good to make a connection with her past. And it especially felt good sharing that memory with this handsome man she was starting to care for. She felt her stomach do a pirouette. They were standing so close together, she could have almost—

She put a stop to that direction of thinking and hoped he couldn't tell she'd actually thought about kissing him.

John looked pensive. "When we were at the Barbours' and they were setting up their tree...that was really nice, wasn't it?" He seemed to be searching for some sort of reaction from her.

"Oh, yeah. It was beautiful." Maggie remembered the special moment that had passed between them at the Barbours's. She also remembered their snowmobile ride and how good it had felt to hold on to him…

She yanked her thoughts back to the moment. "So, are you thinking about getting a really huge tree for that big space?"

His expression was reluctant. "Well, I've definitely let Christmas sort of slide for the last few years and…" He ended with a faint shrug, as if it was too painful to complete the explanation.

She hadn't meant to bring up difficult memories for him. "After what you've been through, John, it's completely understandable."

He brightened. "The kids would love it, though, wouldn't they?"

"Are you kidding me?" Maggie said. "With the energy that they have, they'd have that thing decorated in three minutes flat."

"I'm sure you're right. Hey, I'd like to show you something. There's a vacant office not far from here where I'm thinking about setting up an office. Would you like to see it?"

She was pleased that he wanted to share this with her. "Sure."

"It's this way." He indicated the other side of the street.

Walking side by side, they crossed the street at the crosswalk, though there was no traffic to speak of. Maggie liked the sleepy small-town feel of North Creek. She felt so at home that she wondered if she'd grown up someplace like this.

Don't try to force the memories, she reminded herself.

"I like the idea of the town center for an office location," John said. "It's close to everything, including where the kids go to school. It would be convenient for clients."

"I can see that. But I thought you liked your home office."

"Oh, I do. But as it stands, if an animal needs surgery or even something as basic as an X-ray, they have to go into Boulder, which is an hour's drive at best, and the traffic that way gets worse every day. Can you imagine if Katy had needed an X-ray for her leg?"

Maggie could well imagine, and the idea was awful. "Nancy would have had a long drive with Katy in pain. That would be stressful for both of them."

"Exactly. I'd like to have an office where my patients—and other veterinarians in the county—can come for X-rays and minor surgeries." John stopped at a large one-story building at the corner of the intersection, just down the street from city hall. "This is it. Want to peek in? It's vacant right now."

They peered through the plate glass of the double front doors. There weren't any lights on, but the windows let in enough light to see.

"It's big," Maggie said. "Lots of potential. What was it before?"

A brief frown creased his forehead. "A mom-and-pop hardware shop. The owners were friends of ours. One of those big box stores went up on the outskirts of town. It eventually drove the Millers out of business, and they moved to Florida."

"That's kind of sad," Maggie said.

"Yeah, I agree. But the world changes, no matter how much we wish it would stay the same…" He paused as if lost in thought, and Maggie wondered if he was thinking of Julie.

He cleared his throat. "It would need substantial remodeling inside, of course."

Maggie nodded. "Sounds like you've thought this through."

"I have. Daisy will be in school full-time next year, so I should take the next step." John's words were matter-of-fact, but his voice told another story. He sounded almost reluctant.

Intrigued, Maggie asked, "So, have you put a deposit on this place?"

"No, I haven't pulled the trigger yet."

"Why not?" Maggie asked, hoping to draw him out.

He gave an uneasy shrug. "Something's holding me back. I'm not sure why."

"Someone wise once told me to trust my instincts." She nudged him in the ribs with her elbow. "I think that was good advice. I mean, don't force it. Trust that you'll know when it's right."

"Well said," he answered with a wry laugh. "Who was that wise person who told you to trust your instincts? I'd like to meet this guy."

"Very funny." She shook her head but couldn't help smiling. "So, where to next?"

"How about we browse the shops to get some ideas for the kids, maybe pick up a few stocking stuffers at the five-and-dime."

"The *five-and-dime*? I think I remember that from…an old movie, maybe? Those still exist?"

He spread his hands. "What can I say? It's quaint here."

"Well, I think it's charming," Maggie said. "Like stepping back in time. I can't wait to see the five-and-dime. Lead the way."

After thoroughly exploring the five-and-dime, doing more window shopping, listening to a Renaissance trio sing carols, and watching a glassblower make Christmas ornaments for a street fair, Maggie saw John's optimism, and she found his joy contagious.

"What do you say we grab a bite here in town?" John asked.

"I thought I was going to cook tonight." Maggie realized she'd been looking forward to it. One more thing she knew about herself: she liked to cook.

"Maybe tomorrow. It's getting late, and we haven't even stopped for groceries yet." John waved a hand upward to indicate the sky. "Today kind of got away from me."

It was completely dark already. She hadn't noticed. "But what about the kids?"

"Bunny texted that they got hungry, so she made

a pot of spaghetti. Now they're making popcorn and getting ready to watch a Christmas special."

"I *am* a little hungry." It seemed like she was often hungry. Did she always eat like this and have an extraordinary metabolism, or was the hunger a temporary side effect of her head injury? Either way, she did like food.

"How about this," John said. "We let someone else cook for us tonight. I need to run an errand in the morning anyway, so I'll take your list and stop by the grocery store then. You can cook up a storm tomorrow night."

Tomorrow night. Would she still be here tomorrow, not knowing who she was? That was distressing to think about. But so was the idea that she *wouldn't* be here tomorrow, that she wouldn't be cooking for John and the kids. That she'd go back to some other life and never see them again.

"You're clenching your hands," he said.

She looked down. "You're right. Am I a worrier?"

"Deep breath. Now let it out."

She did, then smiled sheepishly at him.

"Better?" he asked.

She nodded. "What were you saying about dinner?"

"Come on, let me treat you. We'll think about tomorrow tomorrow."

John opened the door to BG Alpen Grill and held it for Maggie.

"Thank you," she said, walking into the restaurant.

"Hi," John said to the hostess. Before he could even request a table, he noticed someone in the main dining area, and said to Maggie, "Oh, hey, it's the sheriff." They went over to the table where he was seated. "Sheriff!"

"John, Maggie," Sheriff Edwards greeted them.

"Hi, Santa," John said to the man sitting opposite the sheriff.

"Maggie, this is my deputy, Darren Wilkes," Sheriff Edwards said.

The deputy was dressed up in a red velour jacket and pants, with gold buttons, a wide black belt, plush white trim, and a matching stocking cap with a white pompon at the tip. He was surprisingly young and smooth-faced for a Santa—thirty, at most, Maggie estimated.

"Oh, is that your uniform?" she asked.

"No, it's my turn to play Santa in the Christmas pageant this year," he said with good humor. "I thought I'd walk around a little. Get into the part. Now, you're that lady who's missing, aren't you? Or maybe I should say you're the one who's been found?"

Maggie cringed inside. Lost and found, that was what she was for now. "Uh, I guess that's me, yeah. So, any news?"

The sheriff answered. "Well, we took your picture and description and put it out over the wire and around town. We also posted it to all those missing-persons sites online."

"Have you seen the poster?" Darren asked, proudly showing her one of the flyers.

Disappointed that no one had responded to the various appeals for information yet, and embarrassed by the picture of herself, she said, "It's not a very flattering photo."

The sheriff looked over the flyer again. "That's... that's not really the point, ma'am." He forced a smile. "Just stay positive. Somebody's bound to come forward."

"Definitely," John agreed. "Thank you, gentlemen. Enjoy."

"Have a nice evening," Sheriff Edwards said.

Maggie sighed. *Stay positive.* It felt like everyone had the same advice for her, but no answers. How could she not be discouraged?

"Honestly," John told Maggie, as they walked away from the table, "after the storm that we've had, things move a little slowly, but I wouldn't worry about it."

She knew he was trying to lift her spirits. So far, it wasn't working.

A pretty woman in a wine-colored sweater came up and interrupted them.

Maggie noted John's instant wariness. Wow, something about this woman really set him off.

"I have seen your face *everywhere*," the woman said to Maggie.

That sounded encouraging. "You have?"

"Yeah. I'm Brooke," the woman introduced herself

with a chuckle. "The sheriff's been putting your photos all over town."

"Oh, okay." So Brooke only recognized her from the flyers? Disappointment returned to Maggie full force.

"But you do look kind of familiar," Brooke added. "Have we met?"

"I don't know. Have we?" Maggie asked, still hoping against hope.

Brooke laughed at her own blunder. "You wouldn't know 'cause you *don't remember* anything."

The woman sounded so amused at the idea of Maggie's amnesia that Maggie couldn't help feeling irritated by her insensitivity.

"That's really stupid of me," Brooke rattled on. "It's like *I* got hit on the head." She laughed at her own joke and gestured awkwardly, as if embarrassed. "Anyways, I know everyone in town, so I'll just keep asking around."

"Thank you," Maggie said.

"Yeah. I mean, anything for Johnny." Brooke gave John a playful shove.

Jealousy flashed through Maggie. Was Brooke really flirting with John, right in front of her? It seemed rude. For all Brooke knew, John and Maggie could be on a date. A similar thought might have occurred to John, because he raised his eyebrows at Brooke.

Crossing her arms, Brooke said, "Okay, bye," and made a hasty retreat.

"See ya," John said.

Maggie gave him a sidelong glance. "*Johnny.*" She teased, and gave him a playful shove, mimicking Brooke.

"That was high school!" he protested.

They went back to the hostess stand and looked at a menu while they waited to be seated.

"What's good here?" Maggie asked.

"What do you like?"

Maggie tilted her head and stared at him, waiting for him to notice his mistake.

"Oh," John said. "Hey, you know what? I have a better idea."

"Better than…?"

"Better than sitting down and ordering off the menu. Since you don't know what you like, will you trust me to pick something?"

She shrugged. "I suppose it can't be any weirder than a bologna omelet. Sure, you choose."

John flagged down the hostess. "We've decided to get dinner to go."

"Sure, John. The usual?"

He nodded. "For two."

"I'll bring it out to you in a couple of minutes." She headed toward the back.

"What's the usual?" Maggie asked. "And where are we going? Back home?" She hoped not, at least for the moment. The day had been so wonderful that she wanted to spend just a while longer alone with him.

He whistled and looked up at the ceiling, pretending to ignore her.

140

"Fine." Maggie plopped down on the bench in the entryway. "I guess I'll just have to trust you."

"You did agree to that," John said, his lips turned up in a roguish grin.

CHAPTER 20

John's palms sweated against the steering wheel as he drove. When he'd decided to take Maggie to his special place, he hadn't realized he'd be nervous about it. What if she didn't like it?

"Are you stressed about something?" Maggie asked.

"Maybe." John felt his face flush and hoped she couldn't see it in the darkness. "Just a bit."

She gave a faint laugh. "I had the impression that you didn't get stressed."

"I have my moments. That's when I come out here." He turned onto an ice-covered dirt road. They bumped along through snowy fields for a few minutes before he stopped the truck and turned off the engine.

"There's nothing out here," Maggie said, sounding wary.

"That's the idea. Quiet. Peaceful." John wanted to open up about himself, share his past struggles. Or he could just let the place speak for itself, but maybe she needed to hear this. Maybe he needed to say it. He drew a deep breath and took the plunge.

"I started coming here after Julie died—late at night when I couldn't sleep and my thoughts got to be too much. Bunny was staying at the house to help with the kids, and she understood. I'm not sure I could have gotten through it without her. And without this place."

"That must have been really hard."

"Still is sometimes," he admitted. "I'd like to show you the rest." He put on a ski cap since they would be outside for a while and got out of the truck. Grabbing a flashlight, a blanket, and their dinner from the backseat, he went around to Maggie's side and helped her get out.

"Watch your step. The ground's icy," he said. He took her hand to stabilize her until they got to the back of the truck. He tried not to think of how warm and smooth her hand felt in his. Holding her hand felt natural, familiar, even though he had never done it before. But right now, he was just a friend trying to help a friend, wasn't he? Best not to let his thoughts roam.

Reluctantly, he let go. Flipping down the tailgate, he pulled out a thick cushion of closed cell foam that he kept in the covered truck bed. He set the food, blanket, and flashlight on it. "We'll sit here," he said. "Is...is it all right if I help you up?" She nodded. He put his hands around her waist, and she put one hand on his shoulder for balance as he boosted her onto the tailgate. He wrapped the blanket around her for extra warmth, then jumped up himself.

When they were situated, he handed her a cup of tomato soup and a grilled cheese sandwich. "This is some of the best comfort food I know," John said. "Well, there's also Ben and Jerry's, but this isn't the best weather for it."

"The ice cream?"

"So you remember Ben and Jerry's!"

She shrugged. "I guess my memory has strange priorities."

Surrounded by snowy fields, they ate for a few minutes in companionable silence.

"This is wonderful," she said. "Quiet, cold, but peaceful. I see why you like it."

"There's more to it than that. Look up there," he said, pointing toward the sky. He watched Maggie's reaction as she tilted her head back and gazed up at the stars.

"It's magnificent," she breathed.

"There's no glow from city lights out here, so you can see the stars much better."

"Sounds like a metaphor." She shivered slightly even though she was bundled in the blanket.

To block some of the cold, he moved closer to her until his jacketed arm pressed against the blanket. "Maggie, I know how hard it can be to lose somebody or something. People say dumb things, like 'Be patient,' 'Don't dwell on it,' 'Stay positive,' or 'Time heals all wounds.' They're trying to help, but they don't live with the constant feeling of loss. Sometimes you need to look right at the pain before you can accept it. And if you get away from the well-meaning people—just for a little while—you can process what happened."

"Like getting away from city lights lets you see the stars?" she said.

"Yeah. There's darkness, but when you look right into it, there are all those tiny sparkles of light, too." It felt so good to have someone sitting beside him who could understand.

"I had no idea there were so many stars." She gave a breathless laugh. "Or maybe I did, but I forgot."

He looked at her. The moonlight reflecting off the snow highlighted her beautiful features. "I know it's tough, not remembering. But I'm glad you can laugh about it."

She turned toward him. "Me too. Thank you."

"For what?"

"For finding me. For taking me into your home. For letting me get to know your kids. And for showing me this. I do feel better." Her contented sigh came out in clouds of white in the winter air.

Their faces were close together, and his puffs of breath mingled with hers as he spoke. "I've never brought anyone else here. I hoped it might help you the way it helps me. But on the way here, I had a few minutes of self-doubt. I wasn't sure you'd see it the same way I do."

Her smile looked brilliant in the moonlight. "How could I not? The quiet, the stars, comfort food—it's like being wrapped in a blanket made of hugs." She gave a soft laugh, the puff of white hanging between them. For a moment, John was mesmerized.

"There's something that could make tonight even better," she said.

"What's that?"

"Some Ben and Jerry's in front of a roaring fireplace."

John laughed. "I think I know where we can find those."

"Should we get enough ice cream for the kids?" Maggie asked. "Do you think they're still up?"

"If I know my kids, they're reading with flashlights while Bunny dozes in the rocker."

When they were back in the truck, John realized a surprising thing had just happened: unprompted, Maggie had asked to include Jamie, Kyle, and Daisy in a special activity.

One reason he had avoided dating was because as an only parent, he didn't want to cut into the time he spent with his kids or make them feel left out of a new relationship. But maybe—with the right woman—he wouldn't have to worry about that.

CHAPTER 21

The next morning, John did his errands in town and picked up the groceries Maggie had requested. Everywhere he went, his mind kept returning to one thought: Maggie. Was the memory of last night under the stars going through her head, too?

When he got home, he brewed some fresh coffee and put groceries away, humming to himself. Jamie, Kyle, and Daisy had been thrilled to get up and eat ice cream together by the fire after bedtime, and Maggie had hugged them all before they went back to bed. She seemed to be developing quite a bond with his kids.

As John finished putting the eggs away, he looked up to see Maggie padding down the stairs. The blanket around her shoulders reminded him of the blanket he had wrapped around her last night as they watched the stars.

"Well, good morning," he said, enjoying her presence. How could he have missed her already when it had been less than twelve hours since he last saw her? He poured her some coffee, which already seemed like a morning tradition between them. "How did you sleep?"

"I don't remember any of my dreams, but today, I don't even care. I'm just going to enjoy whatever the day brings." She sipped from her mug. "Don't forget, I'm cooking tonight. Where are the kids?"

"Having breakfast at Bunny and Emmett's. They're on their way back down now."

The back door banged open, and the kids tromped in.

"Hi guys. I have a surprise for everyone," John said. "How would you like to cut down our own Christmas tree in the forest? My friend at Colorado Parks and Wildlife got us a permit."

"Yeah!" Kyle said, jumping up and down.

"Yay, yay, yay," Daisy said, bouncing with excitement.

"That's the best, Dad. Thank you." Jamie hugged him.

* * *

John and Maggie put on the snow pants and parkas they had worn for snowmobiling, along with duck boots to protect their feet from the snow. Maggie also wore a chunky-knit infinity scarf. The kids bundled up in snow gear, including gloves, snow boots, and ski caps. They all piled into the pickup truck.

"We don't have far to go," John explained. "Antonio gave me a map of the forest areas where we can look for our tree, and some of them are pretty close."

The half-hour drive passed quickly with excited chatter and Christmas carols. *Almost like a family road trip*, John thought. When they arrived at one of the approved tree-harvesting areas, John parked the car, and everyone got out. He liked to use even fun outings like this as learning experiences, so he led a quick brainstorming session for the traits they were looking for in their tree.

"I want a big one," Kyle said.

"We need a pointy top branch for the star," Jamie said.

"What else?" John encouraged them.

"As long as it's fresh, I'll be happy," Maggie said.

She has brought a freshness into our house, John thought, inhaling the crisp winter air. "What do you want the tree to be?" he asked his younger daughter.

Daisy thought for a moment. "Pretty!"

Sweet Daisy, his little idealist, saw the world in simple terms. John chuckled. "I think we have the shopping list for our tree, then."

Maggie picked Daisy up and swung her around.

John hugged Jamie and Kyle. "Okay, let's move out!"

The first part of the tree search consisted mainly of the kids playing tag and running through the snow while John and Maggie followed at a slower pace. Good. No need to be all business. They were here to have a good time.

Maggie was so beautiful walking beside him.

149

Statuesque, with an enchanting smile and flowing blonde hair. A snow angel…

His breath caught for a moment just looking at her. He cleared his throat. "Have you ever made a snow angel?"

"I don't think so. What is it?"

"I'll show you in a little while."

For an hour, they moved from one cluster of trees to another, discussing which one to get. It was good practice for the kids to evaluate the pros and cons of each possibility, but the kids managed to disqualify every tree. Too tall. Too spindly. Uneven branches. Brown spots. Droopy. Too short.

"Will we ever find just the right tree for us, Daddy?" Daisy asked. "I'm hungry."

"You can't rush important decisions," Jamie told her.

"Don't worry. We'll find it," Maggie assured them.

John wondered if they had passed some perfect trees already, and he hadn't noticed. Maybe they just hadn't seen what was right in front of them. Finally, they came upon a promising cluster of fir trees.

Kyle studied the evergreens at the edge, shaking his head. They must have been twenty feet tall. He seemed to give up and started making a snowball.

"Hold it," John said. They had to settle on a tree at some point. He scanned the cluster, quickly evaluating. He saw the perfect candidate, but would the kids agree? "Oh, come on. What about this guy right here?" He pointed at a plump evergreen. "What do you think?"

"Yes!" the children exclaimed in unison.

"I think that's the one," Maggie said.

"You think that's the one?" John asked. "You guys, too?" he asked the kids. He didn't want to chop down a tree if they weren't sure it was the right one.

"Yes!"

"I'm cutting it down. I'm going in! This is definitely the one."

The tree was so full it was hard to get close enough to the trunk to harvest it, but Maggie held aside some branches, and John managed to chop it down with a minimum of scratches to his face in the process. On the way back to the truck, John held the tree trunk while Maggie and Daisy stabilized one side of the tree and Jamie and Kyle took the other. Together, they got the tree loaded in the back of the pickup.

A pretty great day already, John thought. But the kids wanted more time in the snow, and there was something John wanted to show Maggie.

While the kids played tag and rolled big snowballs, John explained to Maggie how to make snow angels.

Her expression was dubious. "We lie down in the snow? On purpose?"

He grinned at her. "You ready?"

"I think so."

"Okay."

They both flopped down onto their backs and began sweeping their arms and legs back and forth in the snow.

"Swing your arms," John encouraged her. "We're

151

going to overlap a little bit." A small bubble of happiness rose inside him every time their hands brushed together. *Our angels touched*, he thought whimsically. However it had happened, something had brought the two of them together, and he was so fortunate to have met her.

Maggie sort of swung her arms, but seemed to have some difficulty moving them through the snow. "This isn't as easy as you would think," she said.

"You got it!" he told her.

She didn't sound convinced. "I do? I don't know. It feels very icy."

"It's beautiful," John said, sitting up and looking at her snow angel. *She* was beautiful, with her blonde hair fanned out on the snow around her face, and her bright smile. "Looks good."

Maggie sat up beside him and looked at her "angel" in disappointment. "Can I do mine again?" She appeared so sad that her angel didn't look enough like an angel.

"No. Yours looks great. Snow angels are not supposed to be perfect," John said. "I see it. I see it."

Maggie seemed to accept his reassurance and relax. A contented look settled on her features. "Gosh. Well, I know I'm not very good at remembering things," she said, "but...this is the most peaceful place I've ever been. Of that, I am sure."

Peaceful? Looking at stars last night had been pretty peaceful. He was surprised she found it peaceful, playing in the snow with the kids around.

A snowball slammed into John.

"It's not always peaceful," Jamie warned. She hurled another snowball and tackled her dad, giggling.

The kids laughed. Kyle threw snow at Maggie.

Hoping she wasn't upset, John looked over at her. He needn't have worried. She laughed, leaned back, scooped up handfuls of snow, and flung them back at their "attackers." Soon, snow was flying in every direction.

"Are you kidding me?" John laughed, pretending to be outraged at the kids. "Are you *kidding* me?" Daisy tackled him, joining Jamie. "Not you, too!" Caught up in the fun, he hugged them to him and flopped back on the ground, not minding if it ruined the snow angel. They weren't meant to be perfect. "Not my little angels!" he yelled, loving every moment. Giggling, the girls continued to throw snow.

Maggie squealed and tossed another handful at Kyle, who fell dramatically onto the snow between Maggie and John.

John was still play fighting with the girls. "Somebody help me!" he shouted, rolling over to his knees. He lifted Jamie in a slow-motion, pro-wrestling-style move and pretended to throw her to the ground, only to set her down gently. As he turned, he caught a glimpse of Maggie, her face lit up with completely unselfconscious delight.

This is so good for her, he thought. *For all of us. Maybe this* is *the most peaceful place she has ever been. And the happiest the kids and I have been since losing Julie.*

CHAPTER 22

Paula's schedule had been extraordinarily busy, considering Christmas was less than a week away. Every day was packed with business lunches, phone calls, and corporate holiday parties. Fortunately, her schedule would let up in a couple of days. At the moment, sitting in her office after most people had gone home was a welcome respite from mail, meetings, and incoming calls. And the view of Manhattan's lights from her office windows during the holidays was enchanting.

Her assistant sorted documents at the worktable beside Paula's desk.

Paula looked beyond the worktable to the *Homestyle* poster on the wall. Jennifer's face stared back at her, larger than life. She still hadn't returned Paula's call. That wasn't like her.

Paula was not in the habit of worrying for no good reason. If everything was truly fine, the friend side of Paula didn't want to intrude into Jennifer's holiday. The agent side of her, on the other hand, preferred to be kept informed. Paula had done her research. Jennifer had arrived in Denver and there had been a snowstorm in Colorado, but that had been days ago. Why hadn't Jennifer called her back yet?

Brad hadn't heard a word from her, either. Paula knew Jennifer wasn't over the moon about the handsome sportscaster, but would she have dropped off the map to avoid him? Each day, Brad searched the internet for news of her and called Paula to give her updates and to find out what she might have learned.

Paula racked her brain for any sort of physical or emotional crisis Jennifer might have been going through. Was there something she had missed?

She dialed her friend's number on her cell phone. Once again, no one picked up, and she had to leave a voice mail message. "All right, Jennifer," she said, "I don't mean to be a nudge since I was the one who sent you away, but you should call me, darlin'. Just to let me know all is well. Okay, sweetheart? Call me."

This situation was starting to set Paul's nerves on edge. If she didn't text or call by tomorrow morning, Paula would start phoning all her friends in Aspen, including her younger brother, who was a publicist for the ski resorts. Somebody had to have seen Jennifer.

CHAPTER 23

M aggie was happy to be in charge of dinner. She'd been cooking for hours. John was out making house calls on a few of his patients. The kids were back from an afternoon at the library with Bunny and Emmett, and Maggie had told Jamie to keep reading, but she'd insisted on setting the table.

"If you're cooking a special meal, I want the table to be special, too," Jamie had said.

So Daisy and Kyle were playing rock-paper-scissors at the breakfast counter while Jamie was busy setting out dishes and decorating the table.

Maggie stirred some homemade gravy, letting it thicken in a pan on the gas stove. John had managed to get all the ingredients she had asked for, and the kitchen was perfect for cooking. Everything had come together so well. She loved the whole experience of being here with John, the kids, Bunny and Emmett, even Dan. Dan arrived a bit early for dinner, and she put him to work chopping vegetables for the salad.

"So, Dan," Maggie said, "how did you decide to move here?"

"Well, I spent fifteen years living in the big city," Dan said thoughtfully. "Some of them were good. But out here, I met a lot of good people, made some loyal friends I can count on. And really," he concluded, "North Creek just seems to be the place I'm supposed to be. Surrounded by people that I love."

The answer made sense to Maggie. It felt *real*. "Thanks for sharing that with me." She opened the oven and retrieved a wide oval serving platter mounded with food so beautiful it could have been on a commercial. "Okay, everyone. Dinner is ready." Beaming, she carried the platter to the dining table.

John came in as she set the platter down. "Wow. I mean, that looks delicious," he said.

"Did you make all this? Like from memory?" Jamie asked.

Maggie grinned. "Yes, I did. I have no idea how I knew how to do it, but I had a lot of fun."

John looked amazed. "Okay, you gotta tell me—what is this?"

"It's a holiday roast with root vegetables," she said.

"Potatoes," Kyle intoned.

"They're not *just* potatoes." Maggie corrected, heading back into the kitchen.

"Oh, man," John said, still marveling at the food. "Look at that."

"*Haricots verts*," Maggie announced, bringing two more dishes to the table. "Which means 'green beans' in French—which means I know French…? And Christmas pudding for dessert."

"Yummy," John said, taking a closer look at the pudding. "You are a really, really good cook. I mean, you've got a serious knack for this."

It felt wonderful to see everyone so excited and to bask in the compliments. "I do?" She knew the answer, but she wanted to hear it one more time.

"Yeah."

She believed him. Looking into his eyes, she agreed with a heartfelt, "I do."

After the kitchen was clean and Dan headed home, the kids went upstairs to get ready for bed. Maggie and John sat at the breakfast bar, enjoying a rare quiet moment.

Maggie noticed Biscuit curled up near John's feet. "You know, for a vet, you don't seem to like animals as much as I would have expected," she said.

John looked at her in surprise. "I *love* animals."

"Exactly," Maggie said. "But you only have one pet. Isn't that kind of unusual for a veterinarian?"

"Well…" John's eyebrows drew together, as if at a sad memory. "We used to have Julie's horse, Aragorn," he said. "But when Julie died, I just couldn't take on the extra work, so we gave him to the Barbours. And we had our yellow Lab, Pixie, too, for a good long time. The kids loved her, so when we lost her to cancer a few months after…" His voice cracked. He cleared his throat. "We lost Pixie a few months after Julie, and the kids were heartbroken. We still have Biscuit, of course, but I can't face getting another pet. The kids have been through enough heartache. I mean, they've asked for another dog or cat, but every time I'm tempted, I think of all the pain they went through, and I just can't do it."

He's lost so much, Maggie thought. His parents, then his wife, and a beloved family pet. She wished she could do something to comfort him. On impulse, she turned toward him, put her arms around his waist, and hugged him.

He pulled her closer and held her. She let herself melt into his embrace, giving and receiving comfort. Maybe losing her memory wasn't so terrible if she had found this. If they had found each other…

He released her and drew away. "I'm just not ready," he said at last in a broken voice.

Are we still talking about pets? Maggie wondered. *Or does he mean something more?*

John leaned back and cleared his throat. "We should call the kids for bedtime stories," he said, his voice rough. Maggie didn't miss that he was including her in the children's routine. She nodded, not trusting her own voice to be steady.

After the kids came downstairs in their pajamas and John read to them, Daisy declared that she wanted Maggie to tuck her into bed and tell her a story. Of course, Maggie couldn't say no.

Since Maggie was staying in Kyle and Daisy's

room, the kids were still sleeping in their play tents in the living room. Maggie barely fit through the door of Daisy's little pink tent. There wasn't enough room inside for an adult to sit up, so Maggie lay down beside Daisy and talked to her. She had a hard time remembering a story, so she told the fairy-tale Sleeping Beauty, with Daisy in the starring role. As she talked, Daisy snuggled up to her and also cuddled her doll, Sally.

At the end of the story, Daisy said, "And now you sing."

Maggie put an arm around the little girl. The situation seemed familiar, but Maggie couldn't quite recall why. Was it just from her own childhood? Or did she have a child? She wasn't sure, but the thought left a dull ache in her heart. Just as she was wondering what to sing, a Christmas lullaby came into Maggie's head, and she sang it.

Santa's sleigh flies all night through.
Bringing joy to me and you.
Make a wish, make a dream.
If you believe, it will come true.

When the song finished, Daisy turned to Maggie. "Where did you learn that?"

Maggie was certain now where the memory had come from. "My mommy sang it to me when I was little."

"Can you sing it one more time?" Daisy asked in a sleepy voice, hugging her doll.

"Sure, sweetheart," Maggie said. This was so familiar. She hoped that tender moments like these were a part of her normal life. If not, she wished that they could be.

Santa's sleigh flies all night through.
Bringing joy to me and you.
Make a wish, make a dream.
If you believe, it will come true.

When Daisy was asleep, Maggie crawled out of the little girl's tent. Not wanting to go too far away yet in case Daisy woke up, she got some paper and sat at the backgammon table, sketching a table decked out for Christmas, complete with place settings, candles, and a beautiful turkey.

Around midnight, John came into the room and set a cup of hot herbal tea in front of her.

"Didn't the doctor say you were supposed to get plenty of rest?" He kept his voice low so as not to wake up the kids in their tents. He stood close beside her chair and leaned over to study her drawings.

Warmth crept into her cheeks, and a smile tugged at her lips. "I just can't help myself. This makes me happy." She realized with a tingle at her core how close together she and John were. For a moment, she couldn't seem to catch her breath.

He turned his face to look at her, and before she knew it, his hand touched her cheek.

A million competing thoughts flashed through her mind. Earlier, he'd pulled away. Why? Maybe his memories of Julie had been holding him back—but now, he was touching her again.

She felt herself falling for this man. But what if it turned out that she was married or had a boyfriend? Or what if she was just imagining things and he was simply being nice? What if she got her memory back tomorrow and he found out she was actually a total jerk?

Or what if she had never felt this way for anyone in her whole life? She gasped in a breath, trying to think.

At her gasp, he let his hand drop, and he stepped away. "I'm sorry. I shouldn't have."

Her cheeks felt furiously hot now. "No, it's okay. I… It was…" *What was it?* she asked herself. *Frightening? Enticing? Exciting?* "It's fine," she finished lamely.

He pressed his lips together and nodded. "All right, then. I'll turn in now. Don't stay up too late."

Maggie hadn't meant to spook him. He looked disappointed and withdrawn. She hoped that tomorrow they could get their signals uncrossed. "Sweet dreams," she said.

"You too," he murmured, and then he was gone.

CHAPTER 24

Maggie woke to Biscuit nosing her face and hand. Dogs were so much simpler to understand than people. They gave affection and wanted affection in return. And maybe some food.

"Hello, Biscuit," Maggie said, stroking her head, enjoying the warm, uncomplicated contact. No mixed messages. There was no doubt about how the dog felt about Maggie. The dog licked her face. "Hello, sweetheart. Good morning."

Even after Maggie put on a long-sleeved sweater, a pair of fleece lounge pants, and some shearling slippers, she felt a distinct chill in the air. Wrapping a blanket around her shoulders, she made her way downstairs. Without waking the children, asleep in their play tents, she knelt in front of the living room fireplace and lit the fire.

Feeling pleasantly self-sufficient, she headed into the kitchen. While the coffee was brewing, she set out mugs, cream, and sugar. She was learning where everything was. Nothing wrong with her short-term memory. "Okay, and...all right."

"Mmm, coffee," John said as he entered the room.

"Yes. It's ready, actually." She took the percolator off the stove.

"Nice. And I see you got a fire started."

"I did," she said, happy he had noticed her efforts.

"Wow."

This was the reaction Maggie had been hoping for. He didn't seem to be dwelling on their miscommunication at the end of last evening. She didn't want to push him away. Just the opposite, in fact. She handed him a cup of coffee, smiling at his compliments. "Here you go."

"Thank you." He seemed about to say something more when Daisy ran into the room, dressed head-to-toe in kelly-green fleece.

"I look like a giant green bean!" Daisy declared. "I'm supposed to be an elf." She hung her head.

"Oh, Daisy. But you're a really cute green bean," Maggie said, trying to comfort her. It was not a flattering outfit, though. Even *Maggie* could do better.

Wait—was that true? She had learned a lot about her abilities in the past few days. Maggie thought carefully. *Make something out of what you have.* Where had that thought come from? A few disjointed images flashed in her mind: her own hands cutting cloth, laying out patterns, attaching buttons, stitching seams. It couldn't hurt to try, could it? "Maybe I can help you," she told Daisy.

Daisy looked up at her with dawning hope.

That did it. Maggie *would* find a way to fix this. "Um, I think I can. I just need"—she turned toward John—"a sewing kit."

She thought she saw gratitude in his eyes as he said, "I think I can find one of those. Come on, I'll show you. We'll have to go outside for a few minutes, though."

Maggie pulled on a pair of boots. She kept the blanket around herself as a layer against the cold. After throwing on a shearling-lined leather jacket and some shoes, John escorted her across the yard to the barn.

They entered through a side doorway with a raised threshold. "Watch your step right there," John said, pointing out the obstacle.

Even inside the barn, the air was so cold their breath came out in white puffs. Maggie pulled the blanket tighter around herself and inhaled deeply. The smell brought an image to mind of digging in a garden—earthy and primal.

"Thanks." She looked around the huge interior. Chinks between the wall boards and the door let in shafts of light. The main bay of the barn was enormous. Massive rolls of hay were stacked three bales high to one side, and a fifteen-foot ladder stood nearby. She looked up and saw a loft, then higher above, the eaves disappeared into the shadows. "Wow, look at this great space."

He put his hands in the pockets of his blue jeans

as they walked further in, looking less relaxed than he had in the house. "Thanks. It's cool, right?"

"Yeah."

"Julie used to keep her horse out here." He indicated the horse stalls on the far wall and stuffed his hands back into his pockets.

That caught Maggie's attention. So, this was Julie's place. That must be why John was tense.

John kicked at a clod of dirt on the barn floor. "I've been wanting to turn it into an animal hospital for a while now. I mean, I'd just love it if my clients didn't have to drive sixty miles to Boulder if their animal needs surgery, you know?"

"Oh, yeah." He appeared pensive now, and vulnerable. Maggie wanted to know more, even though the subject of his wife might be sensitive. "I was actually meaning to ask you about her. About Julie."

John glanced away, and it took him a few moments to gather his thoughts before he spoke in a soft, halting voice. "Oh, um. Well. She passed away a little over three years ago, now. And, uh, she wasn't sick for all that long. Which was good. You know, if anything good could come out of that."

Maggie saw pain on his face as he talked about Julie's death. She hadn't meant to dredge up the unhappy thoughts. "I'm so sorry."

His voice sounded husky now. "Thanks."

Maggie wanted to help him recall happier times. She wanted know more about his past, about what made him the man he was. "But that's not really what

I meant. I…I actually wanted to hear… What was she like?" Maggie looked into his eyes. "Like a memory or something."

He gave a somber nod. "Oh. Okay, um…" Still looking reticent, he dropped his gaze to the barn floor and began to talk again. "She would make freshly baked cinnamon bread every weekend for the family. She loved that. We would make sure to spend time together every evening after the day to talk about how things went, usually over a glass of wine. That was really important to us, to do that."

Maggie noticed his tone was more wistful now than sorrowful. He looked into Maggie's face and she gave him an encouraging smile. He went on in a stronger voice.

"She loved Christmas. I mean, Christmas was her holiday. She just did it up right. Homemade stockings for the kids. She did the handmade ornaments. She would always make sure the kids would get one present that they really, really wanted. And then one present that she felt would make them better people. And every year—I mean just about every year, I think—they would really prefer that present anyway. You know?"

Maggie was amazed at the pride and tenderness in his expression as he remembered Julie. *Has anyone ever cared about* me *like this?* she wondered. If so, how could she possibly forget a love like that?

Without prompting, John shared more in a low voice. "I know this might sound strange, but she just had…she just had a wonderful scent. When I woke up in the morning, even before I opened my eyes, I would just know she was there. I just knew that she was all around me." He hardly looked up as he spoke. Then, as if realizing how much he had said, he cleared his throat and stopped.

Maggie had been immersed in the images, swept away by the love they showed. How very sad it was that John had lost her. Maggie *felt* it. She wanted to let him know that she understood. "Wow. She sounds like an amazing person. You must miss her a lot."

He walked over toward the front wall and began looking around.

Make something out of what you have, a voice inside Maggie said. She had a sudden insight, but she needed to word it carefully. "Hey, you know, if you did turn this space into an animal hospital, then it would be like you were doing something *for* Julie. Like something in her memory, you know?"

His face was serious as he said, "You know, I honestly never thought about it like that. I like that." He seemed to be lost in thought as he searched around for another minute. Finally, he held up a compact sewing box by its handle. "I've got it."

"Great," Maggie said. The three-tiered, accordion-style box was made of wood with decorative carving all around it. Julie's box. "What a neat-looking sewing kit."

John looked at it with a wistful smile. "Yeah." He handed the sewing kit to Maggie, who held it as they left the barn and crossed the yard to the house.

Maggie understood what this box meant. It was a part of who Julie had been, a reminder of the woman who'd made handmade decorations, discussed each day with him, and surrounded his life and their children with love. He had entrusted it to Maggie.

She thought Julie would have approved of using the sewing box to make Daisy's costume.

CHAPTER 25

Maggie set about making a new costume for Daisy with great anticipation. Although Daisy's current costume was a drab green that offended Maggie's eyeballs, that wasn't the main reason she was excited. Maggie's realization that she could probably make a costume had been a revelation, a key to her past. She wanted to know what memories sewing would bring. Maggie carefully disassembled Daisy's "green bean" costume. Then, using a roll of butcher paper that Jamie had lugged up from the basement, Maggie sketched additional pieces for the costume by hand—a belt, a fancy little collar, and for good measure, a hat.

She needed more than just a sewing kit now. She needed materials.

John took Maggie downstairs to the stack of clear bins where Julie had kept all her fabric and sewing supplies. Maggie rummaged through the boxes and came across a piece of red crushed velvet, not large enough for the whole costume, but it was a start. John lifted a sewing machine case down from a shelf, put it at his feet, and stood, watching her. Maggie was delighted by some of the lovely pieces of material she came across, even though they weren't right for this project—gold brocade, black crêpe de chine, sage-green linen, and a cheerful woven cotton sprinkled with blue wildflowers. Pleased that she could coax the fabric names from her foggy memory, she made little sounds as she looked at each one and set it aside, hoping that perhaps she could come back to it at some time in the future. But that would imply she had a future here.

Then she came upon a rich green crushed velvet, not a dull or sickly green. She liked it.

"Aha!" she said, holding it up in triumph.

John grinned. He seemed to be enjoying her little treasure hunt. "Great. Do you need anything else?" His smile was infectious, and she couldn't help returning it.

"Just a few more things," she said, pulling out a piece of felt, a string of gold sequins, and some white buttons. She gathered all her treasures into a smaller bin, closed up Julie's large bins, and stacked them neatly. As she put them away, she noticed another set of bins on a high shelf.

"What's in those boxes up there?" she asked.

"The rest of our Christmas decorations. Decking the halls was mostly Julie's department."

"Should we get them down?"

"Um, sure," he said.

But by the way he hesitated, she could see he was

reluctant. Maggie put a hand on his back. "It's okay. We don't have to if you don't want to."

"Maybe later, then," he agreed.

Picking up her small bin, Maggie started toward the stairs. Thinking of Julie, she turned and said, "The barn really is a wonderful building, you know."

John's expression became thoughtful. "It is. And it holds a lot of good memories. Julie's horse was there, of course, and we boarded other horses for neighbors. Sometimes we stored extra bales of hay for local farmers. Julie gave riding lessons, mostly to kids in the community. She loved it, and the money it brought in helped us pay down my student loans for veterinary school." His face was animated as he thought of these memories.

Again, Maggie wished she could share some memory with him. She felt closer to him, and it seemed only right, but she had nothing to give. Maybe the sewing would yield some insight.

Back upstairs, Maggie laid out her pattern pieces on the various lengths of cloth she had found. She pinned the pattern down and used cloth shears to cut out each piece. Next, she set up the sewing machine. She didn't have to think about what she was doing— her hands just automatically did what they needed to. She was making something out of what she had, and she had *skills*. It only took a couple of hours to sew the pieces together, and she made all the fastenings of the costume with hook-and-loop closures so that dressing would be easy for Daisy. With the basic costume complete, Maggie set about adding embellishments. Each one gave her a deep feeling of satisfaction, and she found herself enjoying this part even more than sewing the costume.

While she worked, she caught flashes of some intriguing memories: sewing beside a woman with short brown hair, making...making a Christmas tree skirt—that was it—and a midnight-blue table runner with tiny gold and silver stars embroidered on it. In another flash, they were making oven mitts. Who was the woman to her—an older sister? An aunt or family friend? Her mother? It frustrated Maggie not to be able to really see the memory, but even the fleeting half memories produced a warm glow that started at the center of her stomach and spread outward.

Late that afternoon, John, Maggie, and the kids went to the town center for the Christmas pageant. They were all bundled up against the cold since the pageant was held outdoors.

John held Daisy's hand as they walked toward the bandstand pavilion. Daisy wore her new elf costume under her parka. He had helped her study her lines for the pageant, and Maggie and Jamie had helped her get dressed and fix her hair.

"Excited?" Jamie asked Daisy, putting a supportive arm around her little sister.

"Yup."

"A little nervous?" Jamie prompted.

What great kids, John thought. He was so fortunate to have a close, loving family. His family seemed happier day by day. He stole a glance at Maggie. She looked happy, too, walking close by Jamie's side, fitting into their lives almost like a family member. Like Dan—but not *quite*.

"I can't wait," Kyle said.

The pageant and tree lighting had been part of their family holiday tradition since Jamie had been a baby, and John was glad they all felt the excitement of being there together.

"You look so cute," Jamie assured Daisy.

"Here we are," John said, delivering Daisy to the small pavilion where Santa and some of her fellow elves were getting ready. "Okay."

He, Maggie, Jamie, and Kyle joined the rest of the crowd waiting for the show to begin. Sheriff Edwards and his wife, Sylvia, stood next to them.

When the pageant finally got under way, John couldn't hide his pride in his youngest child. She was up on stage with a small group of kids and Deputy Darren, remembering everything she was supposed to do. She was younger than any of the others. And definitely the cutest, as far as he was concerned. Her costume put the others to shame—which made him even prouder.

It amazed him how much effort Maggie had put into making his young daughter happy, almost like a mother might. What a kind and caring gesture. Feeling grateful, John leaned over to Maggie and said, "She's an elf among green beans."

Toward the end of the presentation, the children recited, "In Santa's workshop far away, Santa's elves work night and day."

"These little elves make video games," Santa said, in turn.

Daisy stepped forward in her beautiful costume. "These little elves give dolls their names," she said, beaming.

Beside John, Maggie grinned, looking as delighted as any of the parents in the crowd.

John felt so lucky. What great kids he had. Daisy had knocked it out of the park.

Santa continued. "And Santa packs the gifts in his sleigh and takes them to kids on Christmas Day. Merry Christmas. Ho-ho-ho." The audience cheered and applauded. "Don't forget, in one hour is the lighting of the tree. Ho-ho-ho."

John leaned close to Maggie and said, "Her costume really was amazing. Thank you."

She smiled and looked self-conscious. "Aw. I think I might have overdone it a little bit."

John was about to tell Maggie she'd done everything *just right*, when Daisy leapt into his arms, and he caught her. "Hey, there she is!"

"I had the best costume ever," Daisy announced.

"You did!" he said. "You looked so good. Congratulations."

"Thanks, Daddy."

He hugged Daisy to him. "Aw, you're so sweet," he said. "Everybody, great job."

CHAPTER 26

They passed the hour until the tree lighting wandering through the quaint outdoor Christmas market. They ate turkey drumsticks from a street vendor and shopped at little stalls that sold books, Christmas ornaments, spiced cider, blown glass, handcrafted wooden toys, roasted chestnuts, hand-dipped candles, and colorful crocheted scarves and hats.

Watching Maggie and the kids walk from one booth to another, chatting and laughing, John couldn't help having mixed feelings. They were so happy together. It would make it that much harder when it ended. He didn't want to put his children through that. Or himself, if he was being honest. But what could he do now? They already loved her. It was already too late to spare them the pain.

John let each of the kids pick an ornament to put on their tree at home. Afterward, when they stopped at a puppet booth, he sneaked away to the glassblower's stall and returned with a beautiful star ornament that reminded him of the evening he had taken Maggie out to his special spot to look at the sky and talk. He presented the ornament to her.

Maggie gazed at the glass star and held it up. "Even in the darkness there are stars?" she said to John, tears welling up in her eyes. "I know that now. Thank you." A tear spilled down her cheek.

John reached out to brush the tear away, and as he touched her cheek, she pressed her hand to his for a moment. It was such a small gesture, but when he withdrew his hand, it felt empty somehow. To shake the feeling, he glanced at his watch. Almost time for the tree lighting.

John drew the kids away from the puppet booth while Daisy excitedly chattered about how she had learned to make the frog puppet hop.

"Very good," John said to Daisy. "Hey, you just might get it from Santa. Who knows?" Catching sight of the booth run by Open Latte, a local café, he decided they had time for one more stop. "Hey, who wants a hot chocolate?"

"Me!" the children cried in unison.

"They do!" John turned to Maggie. "You want one?"

Maggie grinned. "Oh, no. I…I ate like half a turkey." All three of the kids laughed.

"Okay," John said. "Hey, Kyle, help me out. We'll bring them back, okay, guys?"

"Maggie! Hey, kids," John heard the sheriff call out just as he and Kyle left.

"Hi!" Maggie and the girls greeted the sheriff and

Sylvia warmly as John and Kyle headed for the hot chocolate vendor.

John held Kyle's hand as they walked. He wanted to hurry so they could get back and hear whether the sheriff had found out any new information. They were almost at the hot chocolate stand when Brooke appeared in front of them.

"Hey!" Brooke said.

"Hey," John replied cheerfully. "Hi, Brooke."

"How are you?" she asked with a wide grin.

Their awkward date was water under the bridge, he told himself. He could take a moment for a friendly hello. "I'm great, great. How are you?"

"Look what I found." Brooke giggled and held up a green sprig.

She seemed a bit giddy, and he wondered if she'd had a couple of glasses of Christmas cheer already. Tilting her head with a flirtatious laugh, she held the sprig up high.

"Oh, wow," John said, feeling distinctly uncomfortable. She was definitely tipsy. He tried to keep his tone light. "That's mistletoe. *And* you're holding it up for me." He didn't want to make more out of this than it was. "Here you go." Resigned, he leaned forward to kiss her cheek.

Brooke took his face in her hands, turned it, and kissed him on the lips.

He froze, wondering how to extricate himself from her grasp without being rude. He tried to object verbally, but only ended up making muffled sounds while she held her lips to his. It was only a few seconds, but it felt like an eternity.

It was so inappropriate. He felt his face burning with embarrassment. And his son was standing right next to him! Worse, what if Maggie was watching? He hoped she couldn't see. What would she make of it?

He was too polite to call Brooke on her behavior, but she shouldn't be taking advantage of his good nature. He broke off the kiss, blurted, "Merry Christmas," and hurried Kyle over to the hot chocolate stand.

"Merry Christmas," Brooke called after them. "See you at the Christmas dance!"

Finally, it was time to light the town tree. It was lovely: a twenty-foot fir, decorated with red, gold, and green balls, red bows, gold poinsettias, holly, cream lace, and topped with a gold tinsel star.

Maggie watched the festivities with John and the kids, who each held a cup of hot chocolate. John was so close, but right now, she felt further from him than she had since she first arrived. The kiss she saw between John and Brooke had burst her bubble of holiday happiness. Maggie had so hoped...

Shaking the thought from her mind, she put one arm around Daisy and one around Kyle as they waited.

"Santa." Darren counted down, "Three, two, *one*."

The star on top of the huge tree lit up, and all the branches twinkled with tiny white lights. The gathered crowd cheered and clapped.

"It's so beautiful," Jamie said.

"It's so pretty. Look at all the lights," Daisy said.

"That's beautiful," Maggie agreed, not quite able to summon the same degree of enthusiasm. She didn't want to spoil the wonderful day for them. She knew the kids genuinely cared about her as much as she cared for them. It wasn't their fault she'd let herself believe their father felt the same deepening attachment for her as she felt for him.

"Merry Christmas, merry Christmas," John said to the kids.

"It's really pretty, huh?" Maggie said to Kyle.

John leaned toward Maggie. "Merry Christmas," he said, obviously searching for a response.

She definitely felt a response, yet he seemed completely oblivious to her pain. He didn't realize how much it hurt her to know he belonged to Brooke. How could she have been so wrong about how he felt? She couldn't meet his eyes.

"Merry Christmas," Maggie murmured and gave each of the kids a hug.

By the time they walked back to the truck, the kids were beginning to droop. Daisy held Maggie's hand, and Jamie and Kyle clung to John.

On the way home in the truck, the kids fell asleep. Maggie leaned her head against the door and closed her eyes. Over and over in her mind, she saw John kissing Brooke. It had been such a long kiss. On the lips. The way Brooke had been holding his face in her hands had looked so intimate, not at all like a quick greeting between old friends. The memory burned inside her. She knew she had to talk with John, but she needed a little while to choose her words. She had gotten too attached, gotten her hopes up that he had feelings for her that went beyond generosity and kindness. She couldn't let her foolish daydream continue. She couldn't stay.

Once they got to the house, Maggie helped him get the children out. She carried Jamie inside while John carried Kyle and Daisy. It would have been difficult to get the children into their tents, so he carried them upstairs.

While John put the kids to bed, Maggie sat alone on the couch, going over what to say to him. The knot in her stomach felt like it weighed a ton. There was no escaping the pain, but maybe she could get through this conversation without dissolving into tears.

"They are out," John said, sitting down beside Maggie. When she didn't look at him, he added, "You okay?"

She steeled herself to say the words she had rehearsed in her head. "Oh, John, I have to tell you something. As much as I am having the time of my life here—or as far as I know—I think that, um, I should probably find another place to stay...because I don't want to be selfish and come between you and Brooke."

He looked so surprised. "What?"

"It's okay," she said. "I saw you guys—" Too embarrassed to say the words, she made a kissing sound and mimed hugging.

"Oh!" Glancing down, he gave a half laugh and shook his head. "Maggie, no." He turned toward her on the sofa to meet her eyes. "No, no."

She forced herself to keep going. "It's okay. You know, I just fell out of the sky like some crazy snowflake with no memory. I mean, there's a whole world here that I'm not a part of, and I get that."

"It wasn't a real kiss," he said, looking at her earnestly.

"It looked like a real kiss."

"It, well… I mean, it was a kiss, but it was because of the mistletoe," he said in a rush. "The point is, it wasn't real. I mean, we did go out on one date once, but—"

"You did?"

"We did," he confirmed, "but it was so wrong. It was not right. She force-fed me tofu." His eyes pleaded with her to understand.

"I would never make you eat tofu," Maggie said with mock solemnity. He started to smile, and she went on. "Even if it did make you want to kiss me."

He caught her eye, and then looked down and spoke softly, as he had when he'd shared his memories of Julie with her. "Christmas has not been the same around here for a few years now, and having you here with us, it just… You've made it feel special again."

Maggie could see John was sincere, and maybe a bit nervous, telling her this. "Really?"

"Yeah," he said. "And you *are* part of this family." Then, as if he had revealed too much, he stammered,

"I mean... I mean a part of this *world*, here—our world. And I know you're part of another world, too, and you're going to figure out where that world is, but until you do, I..."

Maggie listened with growing hope as he rushed on, leaning closer to her.

"I guess I'm just trying to say that we would love to have you stay with us here." His hand reached out to touch hers.

"You would?" She felt as if he had found a switch inside her that lit her up like the Christmas tree tonight. She could see the answer in his intense blue eyes. She swallowed hard. He wanted her to stay, and more. Part of her was afraid, and part was absolutely certain of her feelings. Yes, this was what she wanted, too. As if drawn by a magnet, she leaned toward him.

"Daddy!" a little voice called from upstairs. "Can I have some water please? I'm thirsty!"

"Um, I guess there was a little bit too much sugar," John said, though he obviously didn't want to let this moment go.

"Daddy, where are you? I want some water," Daisy said.

"I guess you'd better go," Maggie told him. As he went upstairs, she pulled a throw over herself with a smile and snuggled down on the sofa, using the stuffed bear as a pillow. She closed her eyes, remembering how John had looked at her, how he'd reached out, leaning toward her, before Daisy had called him away. She could almost feel his hand on hers. He wasn't in love with Brooke. He wanted Maggie to stay. She pulled the blanket up to her chin and sighed contentedly. She could get lost in those blue eyes.

CHAPTER 27

T he next morning, when John made breakfast, he worked as quietly as he could because Maggie was still asleep on the living room couch with Biscuit in her arms. While dishing up a batch of pancakes, he accidentally clanged the pan against the counter—and winced at the sound. *That* might have awakened her.

The phone rang, and John answered on the second ring. "Hello?"

"This is Tim Edwards," the voice on the other end of the line said. "Just thought I'd give you an update on your found person."

Maggie padded into the kitchen with a blanket wrapped around her shoulders and listened while he spoke on the phone.

"Sheriff," John continued. "Yeah, what's going on?"

"Would you please let Maggie know that we're doing everything we can to identify her?" Sheriff Edwards said. "We're still searching for a car or a purse or other identifier. And this morning, we added her picture and description to some national registries."

Maggie sat next to John at the breakfast counter.

"Okay, I um, yeah. I will absolutely tell her," John said into the phone. "Great. Thank you. Bye."

"Tell me what?" Maggie asked.

"Well, as of today, they're going nationwide to try to find out if someone is looking for you."

Maggie did not seem to take this as good news. "So no one has called?" she asked. She gave a self-deprecating laugh. "I mean, that means no one actually is looking for me. No friends or family. I mean, it's been *five days*. Maybe I'm really a horrible person and nobody loves me."

She looked so vulnerable, John felt a need to protect her from self-doubt. "No, don't say that. Really. I mean, you can't possibly be the person we have come to know here without really touching people, really connecting to people back when your memory was fine."

Her sad brown eyes looked up at him. "Think so?"

"I guarantee that. They just haven't connected with us." He didn't want to think of someone coming to claim her, to take her back to her old life—away from him and the kids. But that was a selfish thought. How could he not want to end her worry by finding out she had friends and family who loved her? "It'll happen."

"'Kay." She gave a small shrug, looking unconvinced.

Was she worried about what might happen to her if no one came forward? He desperately wanted to cheer her up. "Worst-case scenario, you can always move in here with us," he suggested. It was a serious offer, he acknowledged privately—he really wished she *could* stay. Hoping he hadn't alarmed her, he lightened his tone. "Really make a name for yourself making elf costumes and roasting amazing root vegetables."

She smiled, then pretended to be serious as she answered, "You know they're *not* just potatoes." They laughed quietly together. She seemed comforted to share this little joke with him. Looking away with a shy smile, she accepted his offer. "Deal."

John's heart skipped a beat. She had said yes! She had agreed to stay—if no one came for her, that is. A part of John hoped she would never get her memories back, but he instantly banished the selfish thought.

"Hey, how would you feel about holding the fort for the day?" he asked. "You know, with the kids. I've got to go into town. And if you're not up for it, it's no problem. I mean, I can have Bunny come, but—"

She seemed surprised at the idea. "You would *trust* me with your children?"

"Yeah, of course I would," he answered earnestly. Did she think of herself as a stranger, unworthy of his trust?

"Okay, that would be great. I would love that." She looked genuinely delighted.

"Kids," John called. "What do you think? Maggie's going to hang out with you for the day."

From another room, three voices called out, "Yeah!"

Her face broke into a happy smile at their enthusiasm.

"Yeah, I think they're good with it," John said.

Maggie gave a soft laugh. "Yay."

The kids charged into the room and surrounded John and Maggie at the breakfast bar.

"Maggie!" Daisy said, hugging her around the waist.

John watched Maggie light up and return the hug. The kids would definitely be in good hands.

"Do you have to go somewhere, Dad?" Jamie asked.

"Yeah, I've got to see a couple of patients and run some errands in town."

"Do you need an assistant?" Kyle asked.

"Not this time, buddy," John said.

"When will you be back?" Jamie asked, sounding concerned.

"I'm not sure, but you'll be fine here with Maggie." He rubbed Jamie's shoulder.

"Oh, I know that," Jamie said, looking up at him through her glasses. "It's just that we really want to decorate the tree. Can we at least put our new ornaments up?"

"Of course! Get in the Christmas spirit. Do whatever you guys feel like doing. Just promise me one thing—you won't tire Maggie out."

"We promise!" the kids said.

Even though John was a naturally upbeat person, he was surprised to find himself walking with an actual spring in his step today. For the first time in years, he was truly looking forward to doing a bit of Christmas shopping. The temperature was below freezing, and the light breeze stung his cheeks and his ears in a way that brought back pleasant memories of times with Julie.

He walked around North Creek's main cluster of shops, humming along with the Christmas tunes and enjoying the smell of coffee and baked goods wafting out from Open Latte, the town's largest coffee shop. Unable to resist, he stepped into the coffee shop. At one of the wood-topped bistro tables near the door sat Bill Juarez with a large German shepherd at his feet.

Bill looked up from his newspaper with a grin. "John!" The dog's ears pricked up, as well, and he sat up. "Go on," Bill said, and the dog walked over to John and greeted him with a wagging tail.

"Mauser," John greeted the dog, patting his head. "Looks like that eye infection cleared up just fine, huh, buddy?"

"Rita, look who's here," Bill called to his wife.

"I see him." Rita came around the bakery counter and handed John a steaming cup of pumpkin spice latte. "Here. It's on the house."

John was touched by her kindness. Pumpkin spice latte had been a seasonal favorite of Julie's. Between Thanksgiving and New Year's every year, they had come to the coffee shop at least twice a week to share a cup.

"What brings you down this way, Doc—a sick pet?"

John took a sip of his latte. "I thought I'd get in some Christmas shopping."

"Oh," Rita said with a knowing look. "One thing each kid really wants and one thing that will make them better people, right?"

John nodded. "I'm not as good at this as Julie was, but I think I'm doing better this year. I've got some good ideas."

"Are you coming to the Christmas dance?" Bill asked. "You know our granddaughter Sherrilyn's going to be singing with the band."

Mauser wagged his tail furiously and rubbed against John's leg. John pulled up a chair beside Bill's, sat down, and patted Mauser while he drank his coffee.

"Little Sherri?" John teased. "Why, she can't be more than twelve, can she?"

Rita chuckled. "Nineteen years old last month. She goes to CU Boulder now, but she's home for the holidays."

John shook his head. "They seem to grow up so quickly you can hardly keep track of it."

After saying his goodbyes, John's next stop was one of the kids' favorite stores, Deb's Treehouse: Science, Music, and Wonder for the Child in All of Us. After an hour or so, he found exactly what he was looking for. For Daisy, a children's toolbox, complete with hammer, screwdriver, pliers, safety glasses, gloves, level, tape measure, and wrench. The rest of her gift was that he would build a dollhouse with her for her doll, Sally.

For Kyle, he picked out a refractor telescope with a stand. John's time stargazing with Maggie had reminded him of what an important time that could be. He would teach Kyle constellations and try to share at least one evening a week on the telescope with him.

Jamie's gift was a microscope. She thought she might be interested in being a doctor, so he would show her the types of things he looked for when studying a sample. It came with tweezers, a plastic scalpel, glass slides, and a book full of suggested experiments. He'd encourage her to trade time with Kyle so that he could use the microscope and she could use the telescope.

Pleased with his choices, John moved on to another shop, for one last special gift.

CHAPTER 28

At first Maggie wasn't sure how to spend a day
alone with the kids, but a plan soon formed in
her mind. She wouldn't think of telling them to go
watch television and entertain themselves. No, she
had a much better idea.

The tree they had chosen together, chopped down,
and brought home still stood mostly naked in the
front entryway, and the kids wanted to hang their new
ornaments. John had said to get into the Christmas
spirit, so why not do it up right?

"Would you like to add more decorations?" she
asked the kids. "I saw some in the storage room, but
I'm not sure if we should use them."

Daisy tugged her hand. "Yes, let's go get them."

"We should definitely use them," Jamie confirmed.
"We have *lots* of decorations."

"Boxes and boxes," Kyle added.

Maggie let them drag her down the stairs to the
storage room next to their father's office. She handed
a bin of Christmas lights to Jamie and smaller bins of

ornaments to Kyle and Daisy. Maggie carried a couple of larger bins, and they all trooped back up the stairs. It was fun watching the kids open the boxes and sort through them, finding their favorite items. Maggie went and got the short stepladder she had seen in the pantry, brought it into the living room, and set it up by the tree. Pulling a long strand of lights from a box, she started to unwind them. "Wait, there's something missing," Maggie said.

"Sally!" Daisy said, running to get her doll.

"Not quite what I meant, but okay," Maggie said.

"Hot dogs?" Kyle ventured.

"Delicious, but not necessary for decorating."

"Music?" Jamie asked.

"That's right—music," Maggie said.

Jamie showed Maggie a shelf full of CDs and pointed to a row. "These are all the Christmas ones."

Maggie chose an instrumental one by Trans-Siberian Orchestra, and Jamie put it on the mini stereo in the kitchen. "There. Now we have everything we need."

They went back into the living room. After laying out several strands of little white lights, Maggie chose one and had the kids help her put it on the tree. She stood on the ladder, adjusting the placement while they walked the strand around the tree. They hung up every last string of lights they could find. They even turned one of the strings into a kind of bead curtain between the living room and the dining room.

When they hung red and gold ball ornaments

on the tree, Maggie gave each of the kids a turn on the stepladder to hang a few. She guarded each of them while they were on the ladder, and held Daisy tightly while she put up her ornaments. They added filigree ornaments, gold ribbon, gold snowflakes, gold poinsettias, and deep red silk roses.

"This fir tree is wonderful," Maggie said, "but we can make the house smell even more like Christmas. It's time for cookie dough."

The kids cheered. Biscuit woofed.

Jamie put her hair up in pigtails, and Maggie helped Daisy pull hers back in a half pony. They worked at the center island of the kitchen, gathered around it. Daisy sat on one of the high chairs borrowed from the breakfast bar so she could see more easily.

"First, let's collect our ingredients," Maggie said. "We'll need flour."

Kyle went to the pantry and came back lugging a huge plastic bin full of flour and set it on the counter.

"Then sugar, vanilla, eggs, baking soda, and cinnamon."

The kids took turns getting the ingredients. Maggie had Daisy bring the smaller things and those that were easily within reach. Maggie had Jamie crack the eggs while she showed Daisy how to measure ingredients with a teaspoon. Kyle enthusiastically used the cup measure to scoop flour out of the bin. He tried to level the measuring cup by shaking it, and soon, they were all dusted with a fine white coating. Some of the flour even fell on Biscuit, who shook herself vigorously, sending more flour into the air.

When the dough for the chocolate chip snowmen cookies was finished, they put it in the refrigerator to chill while they mixed gingerbread batter. In the process, there were slips and spills and trips and goofs and lots of laughter. Biscuit made herself useful by licking up the spills that reached the kitchen floor. The aroma of the cinnamon and ginger and other spices was heavenly.

Maggie poured the gingerbread batter into shallow jelly roll pans to bake. While it was in the oven, she made homemade macaroni and cheese for lunch. Afterward, she pulled the gingerbread out and set it on a rack to cool. They cleaned the kitchen, and then it was time for crafts.

In front of the living room fireplace, Maggie sat with the kids and showed them how to make their own decorations to add to the ones they had already put up. "Christmas doesn't have to be expensive," she told them. "You can always make something out of what you have." As she spoke, the words had a familiar ring, and Maggie wondered if her mother had said them to her.

Maggie and Jaime folded white paper and cut it into snowflakes while Daisy and Kyle made chains out of red and green construction paper. Biscuit was curled up next to them on the rug. To Maggie, the world felt serene.

"Mom would have loved this," Jamie said with a happy sigh.

"Yeah?" Maggie said. It felt good to hear Jamie say it. "What was she like, your mom?"

"She liked to laugh a lot," Jamie said. "And play music."

"Her hair always smelled like toast," Kyle said.

Maggie smiled at this description. John had mentioned that Julie had a wonderful scent.

"I'm too little to remember," Daisy said, hanging her head, and Maggie's heart went out to her.

"And she liked to make everything nice," Jamie continued. She looked at Maggie. "Like you."

"Yeah. My mom used to make things, too." Maggie said. "I feel like that's how I know how to make all this stuff. Because of her."

"Do you remember your mom?" Jamie asked.

Maggie thought about the question, searching her mind for memories. Although she found nothing clear, she did manage to summon a brief image of an older woman's face and a few stuttering scenes of them doing things together like baking, singing, and opening gifts. It was almost as if she were watching bits of her past lit by a strobe light—there one moment and gone the next. Still, something about the love she felt when she saw the woman's face in her mind convinced Maggie that it must be her mother. She finally answered Jamie's question. "Yeah, you know what, I think I'm starting to."

"I did it!" Daisy exclaimed, holding up a paper

chain she had stapled together. Maggie gave her an encouraging nod.

"I was in town the other day," Maggie continued in a dreamy voice. "I saw these beautiful red mittens in a shop window, and they looked just like this pair that mom made me when I was"—Maggie choked up—"a little girl. So, yeah. Yeah, I remember her. You know what? I think that you and I both had really great moms. That's what I think. Okay, let's see how this one came out." She began to unfold the paper snowflake she'd been cutting.

Jamie unfolded her paper, too. "This is my..." She burst out laughing—it looked nothing like a snowflake.

"You just gotta cut like little parts of it," Maggie explained, "not like all the way through, 'cause otherwise, you kind of cut all the connective tissue." She held up her perfect paper snowflake.

"Ta-da," Kyle said, finishing his paper chain.

Maggie smiled at him. "Who wants to help me make a gingerbread house?"

"Me!" all three kids cried.

"All right, come on."

"Come on, Biscuit. Come on," Daisy said.

When everything was cleaned up, they changed into Christmas clothes to surprise John when he got home. Maggie brushed out Daisy's and Jamie's hair and put it up into matching half ponies. They all wore red Christmas sweaters with white Santas on them that Bunny had dropped by earlier in the day. She had bought the sweaters on a year-end closeout for herself and the kids to wear at Christmas, but she had confided to Maggie, "I think mine might look better on you." Maggie was touched by the gesture. It felt as if Julie's mom was trying to make her feel included in the family. A sense of love and acceptance washed over Maggie, warmer than any sweater.

CHAPTER 29

A light snow fell while John shopped. Enjoying the weather, he put his bags of Christmas gifts in his truck. Across the street, the city hall building caught his eye, reminding him that he needed to make a decision. After a brief hesitation, he shut the door of the truck and crossed the street.

Ever since Maggie had suggested that turning the barn into an animal clinic would be a way to honor Julie, the thought had been working its way deeper into John's mind. It made sense. Changing the building would not take away from the memories he had of Julie. In fact, as he reflected on it, he saw that, for years, he had mostly avoided going out to the barn because it was *empty* of her, of what she would have used it for if she were still alive. How could he honor his wife's love of children and animals and *life* by leaving the barn vacant, like a haunted house?

He entered city hall and went to the reception desk at the center of the lobby. To his surprise, Brooke was working there, even though it wasn't her usual position.

"Brooke. Hi," he said.

She turned to him, looking pleasantly surprised. "Hi! What brings you here? I mean, there's no mistletoe, you know," she said with a chuckle, indicating the empty air over her head.

"Oh, yes, that's true." John grinned, trying not to think about the awkward kiss Brooke had maneuvered him into at the Christmas pageant. "Uh, well, I changed my mind, and I'd like to go ahead and file for those permits for reconstructing my barn."

"Ah, well, that's too bad," Brooke said, her smile not as bright now. "It would have been nice to have your office in town. You know, maybe we could have… had lunch."

"Oh, yeah. It's true." This conversation was going in the wrong direction entirely, and John didn't want to extend it. It had been hard to convince Maggie that there was nothing between him and Brooke. He didn't need to add fuel to the fire.

"Let me get the forms and email them over to the county office," Brooke said.

Before she could leave, a mail carrier walked up to the reception desk and plopped a small bundle of mail on the counter in front of her, and she thanked him. John watched her quickly flip through the stack—some registrations, bills, advertisements, and a cooking magazine called *Aroma*—before turning her attention back to him.

"But are you going to go to the holiday party at the

community center?" she asked. "'Cause I'm serving the punch." She leaned forward with a flirtatious laugh.

He groaned inwardly. He wasn't sure Brooke understood that there was no romance brewing between them. "Yeah, I wouldn't miss it. I'll see you there," he said with a polite smile.

"Okay, good," Brooke answered.

John hurried out of city hall. In spite of the awkwardness of having to see Brooke, getting the permit process started had been easier than expected.

John arrived back at the house carrying several shopping bags full of Christmas gifts. He put the bags on the floor by the front door and called out, "I'm home!"

Walking into the living room, he heard a giggle and stopped, stunned at the sight before him.

Maggie and the children jumped out from behind the fully decorated, fresh Christmas tree.

"Surprise!"

They all looked so cute dressed in matching red Santa sweaters.

"What?" John whispered, gazing in disbelief around the room. Instead of giving a half-hearted nod to the holidays, every corner of the room now glowed with Christmas spirit. Until today, only a room decorated with love by Julie had ever made him feel so simultaneously peaceful and elated. The kids ran to him and hugged him, and he looked across at Maggie. "Oh my…"

"What do you think?" Maggie asked, looking uncertain.

"Dad, what do you think?" Jamie pressed.

He let himself absorb the atmosphere. "I think it's beautiful. I think it's magical. It reminds me of the way things used to be." He had expected any reminder of past Christmases to bring an ache to his heart, but instead, the decorations brought back memories of the joy that came from a house filled with love. "You guys, this is the best surprise ever." He hugged all three kids to him and kissed the tops of their heads.

"And we couldn't have done it without Maggie," Kyle said.

"Yeah," John said, gazing at Maggie with wonder.

"Oh, the cookies!" Maggie exclaimed and ran for the kitchen.

"Oh, the cookies," John happily repeated to the children, taking off his parka as he admired the tree up close. "You guys, this is amazing. Look at this."

Leaving the kids by the tree, he went to the kitchen to tell Maggie how grateful he was.

"I really need to thank you for that," John said. "I mean, it's amazing, and it means a lot to me."

"Well, I should be thanking you. I mean, while I was cutting the snowflakes and making the gingerbread houses with your kids, I started remembering something we used to do with my mom when I was a kid at Christmas." Maggie's face seemed to glow as she shared her memory. "We used to make these little homemade cardboard ornaments where we'd fold the cardboard into little boxes, and then we'd cover it with foil and then put glitter shapes of a Christmas tree or a cross or a star. And the house would always smell so delicious, like gingerbread, and there'd be Christmas music playing. And I remember all that. And I remember"—Maggie's voice broke—"my mom. And I know it's from a really long time ago, but it's a really beautiful memory. It's coming back. So thank *you*."

"That's great!" His heart stuttered. She was remembering. And with every little bit Maggie remembered, the closer he came to losing her. He wanted her here—he couldn't deny it. But that was a selfish thought. She wanted her memories back. If he cared about what was best for her—and he did—he had to root for her to succeed. *Be strong. Be happy for her.* "I mean that's...that's *really* great."

She became even more animated as she spoke. "Yeah, you know, I've been so focused on like 'who am I' and 'where am I going?' And 'I have to figure that out right now.' But this is all kind of so good feeling and happy, and I'm just wondering—maybe I could just forget all that for a few days and just enjoy Christmas?"

He hadn't lost her yet. John held on to that. She felt happy with them. She wanted to be here as much as he wanted it.

She sounded hesitant, but hope sparkled in her

eyes as she said, "Would…would that be all right with you?"

He started toward her, wanting to swing her up into his arms to show her how "all right" it was with him. How could she doubt it? But he didn't want to overstep. He held back and put all his happy relief into his words. "Yeah, that's okay. I would really like that." *She asked to stay with the whole family*, he reminded himself, *not just you.* He quickly added, "I mean, I think—we would *all* love you to stay for Christmas."

She beamed back at him, then glanced down as if suddenly feeling shy. "Great. Thank you."

He took a step closer, struck again by how lovely she was.

"Where are the cookies?" Jamie said, rushing into the kitchen.

John turned and playfully blocked her. "Oh, there's no cookies," he teased. "I don't know what you're talking about."

Laughing, she dodged, and he let her get past him to grab a chocolate chip snowman.

Whisking the rest of the cookie plate out of her reach to save for later, he pretended to be shocked. "You don't like chocolate chip cookies, do you? Walk away from the cookies! Walk away from the cookies!"

"Wait," Jamie said to Maggie. "You're coming to the party tomorrow night, right?"

"What party?" Maggie asked.

"Oh," John said. "Every year there's a big Christmas party at the community center. It's a lot of fun. There's a band. There's dancing." Now that he knew she planned to stay through Christmas, he very much wanted her with him at the party. He hoped it would appeal to her. He spread his hands. "I mean, everybody from North Creek will be there."

Apparently, Maggie didn't need to be convinced any further. "Oh, that sounds like fun. Do I need to dress up?"

"Yeah," Jamie said emphatically and took a bite of her snowman cookie.

Not wanting her to feel pressured since she didn't have a full wardrobe to choose from, John said, "You don't *need* to dress up. You always look great."

Maggie gave a shy smile and glanced down again.

Even though John was trying to be helpful, Jamie took him by the arm and turned him to face her, looking for all the world like a parent lecturing a stubborn child. "It's nice to dress up. Okay?"

"O-*kay*, the serious look there," John said, feeling thoroughly chastised. "I get it. Wow." He glanced at Maggie. She would look beautiful in anything, but he'd make sure Bunny found her something festive to wear.

When he and Maggie came back into the living room, John noticed Kyle looking mischievous, hiding something behind his back.

"Cookies here," Maggie said, holding out the tray she carried.

"Yes," John said, looking around the room full of decorations and lights.

Kyle pulled a large foil-covered star out from behind his back and held it up proudly. "Maggie said we should save the star for *you*."

"She did?" John thought back to that day he'd taken Maggie on the snowmobile to visit Stan and Holly and their kids. The Barbours had put the star on their Christmas tree in a heartwarming family moment. He and Maggie had shared that special moment, and he was touched that she wanted to share a similar experience with his family. He turned to look into her beaming face, then he ruffled Kyle's hair. "Thanks, buddy. Hey, how 'bout I boost you up, okay? You help me."

"Okay."

"Here we go—up you go." John lifted Kyle to sit on his shoulder.

"Woo-hoo!" Kyle said.

"All right. Let's see if you can reach it up there." John inched closer to the tree. "Do your best. Good? You all right?"

"Yeah," Kyle said, placing the star atop the tree.

John put him back on his feet. "Okay, let's check that out."

"Nice job," Maggie told Kyle.

"Thank you."

"That looks great," John said, standing close beside Maggie. He looked into her eyes, and there it was, that same feeling of family and togetherness they had experienced at the Barbours'.

"It's what we needed," Jamie said with a happy sigh.

"Mm-hm." John couldn't have agreed more. He and Maggie looked at the tree, standing so close her shoulder touched his chest, setting off a warm glow that wrapped itself around his heart.

CHAPTER 30

New York was overcast, a fitting reflection of Paula's mood. Brad sat on the leather sofa in her office, looking rumpled and equally disturbed. Neither one of them was used to being ignored. Jennifer *wouldn't* ignore them. But she hadn't returned any of their messages. She was normally so conscientious. She wouldn't just *not call*. She always met her obligations. It was completely unlike her to drop off the radar like this.

In frustration, Paula dialed Jennifer's cell again, which went immediately to voice mail. "All right, Jennifer," Paula said, "you've got me *really* worried now. But you need to call me back. Now." She hung up and turned to Brad, who was intently listening to his phone. "Anything?"

He pulled the cell away from his ear. "Nope. No answer from the chalet." He put his phone down.

"She hasn't made it to the spa, either. I am extremely concerned." Paula had called every conceivable phone number and contact in Aspen, even her brother, Martin. No one had seen or heard anything of Jennifer.

Brad stared down at his phone and started dialing. "I'm going to call the airline. It's time we get on the plane."

Paula was glad she had a clear calendar until Christmas Day. If she and Brad had to fly to Colorado to track Jennifer down, that's exactly what they would do. At this time of year, it might be hard to get airline tickets, but they wouldn't take no for an answer.

CHAPTER 31

Maggie and John sat in the living room, reading and enjoying the ambience of a low fire in the fireplace, Christmas decorations all around them, and a plate of fresh-baked cookies on the coffee table. Maggie flipped through a few magazines Bunny had brought her while John caught up on issues of JAVMA—the *Journal of the American Veterinary Medical Association.* The kids were scattered in different rooms, entertaining themselves: Jamie with a book, Daisy with her dolls, and Kyle with a toy glider.

Maggie heard a knock at the front door.

John got up and answered it. "Brooke! What a surprise. What's, uh…" He seemed to be fumbling for something more to say.

Maggie was surprised, too—even more so when Brooke swept right past John into the house without waiting to be invited in.

"Wow!" Brooke gasped, looking around at the decorations. "Did you do all this?"

"No. No, no, no," John said. "I just cut down the

tree. Maggie and the kids did everything else. What, uh... What brings you out here?" He scratched his nose.

"Oh, I, um..." Brooke said, as if just remembering the reason for her errand. She tilted her head and smiled up at John. "I brought the paperwork for the barn remodel. I just need a couple more signatures, and then I can send it back." She ended with a flirtatious toss of her hair.

Maggie felt a flicker of jealousy. Not only was Brooke flirting with John, he had talked to her about renovating the barn. Maggie picked up a serving plate of cookies, hurried over, and gave John a look of surprise. "So, you're doing the barn?"

Brooke did not look thrilled that Maggie had joined the conversation.

"Yeah," John said.

"That's fantastic." Maggie had encouraged John to turn the barn into an animal clinic.

So why had John had told Brooke about the barn remodel without mentioning it to Maggie? Had he gone to see her at city hall when he was in town today? Maggie felt a jab of disappointment, but plastered a smile on her face.

John glanced down and studiously reviewed the paperwork he held.

During an awkward silence, Maggie wondered if it was normal for Brooke to just drop by unannounced. Was it possible that John cared for Brooke more than he was letting on? Maggie tried to look at the other woman impartially, as John might. She seemed intelligent, was pretty and single, lived in the area, and apparently, had a good job. And the fact that Brooke had hand carried John's paperwork to his house showed she cared for him. Jealousy flickered inside Maggie, and she tried to ignore it.

Quick footsteps thunked across the hardwood floor in the living room.

Brooke turned toward the source of the sound as Kyle ran up to them, zooming a balsa wood glider through the air with one hand.

"Oh, hey, little Kevin!" Brooke said with an exaggerated smile and a giggle.

Oof, Maggie thought. *Not only did she get his name wrong, she called him* little. *He's not going to like that.*

"It's *Kyle,*" Kyle said in exasperation.

"Oh," Brooke said.

Maggie couldn't suppress a smile. John's kids meant the world to him, so Brooke probably wasn't winning any points as a potential stepmom right now. As Kyle left, Maggie caught his eye and winked at him.

"It's really nice of you to bring this all the way out here," John said to Brooke. "Thank you."

Maggie extended the plate of cookies to Brooke. "Would you like a chocolate chip snowman?"

"They're really, really good," John said.

Maggie wondered if he was trying to soothe her with compliments to counteract the unsettling effects of Brooke's visit.

"They're gorgeous," Brooke observed, taking a

cookie. She gave Maggie a curious look. "You know, I...huh. I know I know you from somewhere."

Maggie didn't get her hopes up. Brooke had made the same sort of vague comment the first time they met, and it had turned out she'd only seen Maggie's picture on the flyers around town. Not exactly helpful.

Brooke stared at Maggie a moment longer, then shook her head. "I just can't... Oh, well." Brooke dismissed the idea with a chuckle.

John handed Brooke the signed paperwork.

She hesitated, then said, "Yeah."

"Well, thanks a lot for bringing them out." John grasped Brooke's elbow and ushered her toward the front door.

"I love what you've done with the place," Brooke said over her shoulder to Maggie.

"Yeah, doesn't it look good?" John opened the door and steered Brooke out with a friendly pat on the shoulder. "We'll see you at the party tomorrow night, okay?"

Maggie frowned. So Brooke would be at the party, too.

"Um, sure. Okay," Brooke said.

"Safe drive," John added, starting to swing the door shut.

"Bye," Brooke said.

"Bye." John closed the door. He turned to look at Maggie, and she could see in his expression that he knew she was upset.

She didn't *want* to have this scrambled feeling

of doubt, but there it was. Brooke was obviously captivated with John. How could Maggie believe there was nothing between them? He had contacted her about the barn, and there had been that kiss at the Christmas pageant.

But if Maggie asked John, she knew he would deny that he and Brooke were attracted to each other. It wouldn't help. It would only confuse her more. Even though she wanted to believe him, to trust him completely, something held her back. And always at the back of her mind was the question of whether *she* was already committed to someone else. What would happen when her memories returned? Her stomach churned, and she needed time to compose her thoughts.

She turned and walked away.

"I'll have a cookie," he called after her. His voice was hopeful, as if he thought the two of them could take up where they had left off before Brooke's visit.

She continued walking.

After resting and thinking upstairs for a while, Maggie came back down. She heard John talking on the phone in the kitchen.

"Yeah, thank you. Bye," he said and hung up.

With more than a little hesitation, Maggie entered the room. She wanted so badly to get past this uncertainty, to resolve the tension between them, but she didn't know how.

John looked up. He was dressed in a gray flannel shirt with rolled-up sleeves over a gray tee and jeans. His face brightened when he saw her. "Hey."

"Hi," she replied in a neutral tone.

John's voice was upbeat as he said, "That was the sheriff. He feels like he's getting closer and might even know something tomorrow."

"'Kay. I guess we'll find out tomorrow then." Maggie didn't take much cheer from his report. It had been the same old story every day. What did it even *mean* that they thought they were close? Either they had found something, or they hadn't. They made positive-sounding pronouncements, but when it came right down to it, there was nothing to report. How often could they tell her the exact same thing and expect her not to notice?

John nodded. "I guess so."

She looked across the kitchen at him, feeling as if they were much farther apart than a mere five or six yards. It was hard to admit, even to herself, that seeing John with Brooke had sent pangs of jealousy through her—it was an unattractive, unfamiliar feeling. But she couldn't seem to put it behind her.

He must have noticed Maggie's guardedness. His eyes held hers, and he seemed about to say something.

"Knock, knock," a voice called. The door opened, and Dan came in. "What's for dinner?" He took off his coat. "Hi, Maggie."

"Hi, Dan." Her voice was subdued, but she smiled

and waved to him. For now, she had a reprieve from talking to John about Brooke.

After dinner, John couldn't get his mind off Maggie and how upset she seemed. The comfortable camaraderie they'd enjoyed had been all but ruined by Brooke's appearance. He wanted so badly to clear the air, but he hadn't been quick enough to broach the subject before Dan arrived for dinner. He'd tried to catch Maggie alone in the kitchen while they were doing the dishes, but she'd avoided meeting his eye and had headed upstairs immediately after.

Now Dan sat across the backgammon table from him, still eating. John absently petted Biscuit, who was sitting on his lap. His heart wasn't in the game. Even the dice seemed to sense his lack of enthusiasm. He rolled a one and a two, and moved his pieces on the board while Dan pulled pasta into his mouth.

"Aw," Dan said.

"What?" John asked, wondering at the disappointment in his friend's tone.

Dan pointed at the board with his fork. "You just handed me that. Where's your mind at?"

John held his head in his hand. Trying to act like everything was normal wasn't working. It hadn't helped with Maggie, and it certainly wasn't fooling Dan. "I'm sorry. I'm thinking about Maggie, actually." He raised his head again, but his eyes couldn't focus on anything beyond the thoughts swirling in his mind, as he tried to explain his distraction. "It's so interesting. Because she says that she's happy here. And I know it's been nuts, but I love having her here. The kids love having her here."

"That's all good," Dan said and waited for John to go on. He took another bite.

John wrestled with the real crux of the problem. He dreaded saying it out loud, yet there was no escaping the issue. "But it's going to end," John said. "I mean, she's going to figure out who she is and where she's from, and then she's going to go back there." He scratched Biscuit's head. "So...so what do I do?"

Dan forked a bite of pasta into his mouth and chewed thoughtfully. "When I was nine years old, out behind my daddy's barn, I found a baby rabbit. I brought it in, and I bottle fed that little guy for six weeks. And one day my momma says to me, if I loved something, I had to let it go and see if it came back. I went outside, set it down, and..."

John gestured for Dan to finish the story. He needed to know what happened next.

Dan nodded and smiled. "It hopped away. And I never saw that bunny again."

That was not at all what John had expected him to say. "*Dan*. Are you comparing Maggie to a baby rabbit? What?" He had been looking to Dan for encouragement, a ray of hope.

"No, of course not. I'm saying everything happens in its own good time. If someday she has to leave, then she has to leave. It's enough to just be happy right now. Just be happy now. It's the hardest thing you ever do."

John petted Biscuit again. Dan hadn't exactly given him hope. But it was sound advice.

Upstairs, Maggie pushed aside her thoughts and worries about John while she tried on clothes in front of the mirror in Daisy and Kyle's room. At John's request, Bunny had brought a stack of dresses for her to choose from. She held them up in front of her and looked in the mirror, asking Bunny's opinion about color and length.

She tried on a long gown of gold velvet first.

"Julie's sister Lisa wore this one at a formal dance once," Bunny said. "That looks just lovely on you. It's a shame Lisa won't be home for Christmas this year, what with her trip to London and all. I think she'd really like you."

The comment warmed Maggie's heart. She hoped that if she ever met Lisa, they would become friends. She turned to look at herself in the beautiful gown, smoothing her hands over the rich material. She cocked her head to one side. "Maybe *too* formal?" she asked.

"I think so," Bunny agreed.

She tried on a blue chiffon cocktail dress and a red, tea-length tulle gown, but neither of them felt right to Maggie. In the end, she chose a jade-green semiformal dress with an empire waistline and a bodice decorated with rhinestones and soutache, so it didn't even need a necklace. Bunny stood behind her, looking over her shoulder. They smiled at each other in agreement. With a warm rush, Maggie realized that trying on clothes with Bunny reminded her of similar times with her own mother.

"Ah, I used to wear this on Christmas when I was dating Emmett," Bunny reminisced. "It is so pretty on you."

Maggie loved the color, the vintage material, and the special memories attached to it. "Oh thanks, Bunny. It's...it's beautiful."

"Of course, sweetheart. You know, now that our Julie is no longer with us, the holidays have been a little bit...*different* around here. Still nice, but different. But this year, well, it's feeling like Christmas again. It feels good."

What a gift to know that Bunny believed that Maggie had enriched their lives. Yes, it did feel good, and Maggie's intuition told her that in her other life, she didn't always experience this feeling of wonder. "Christmas is beautiful, isn't it? Getting to be with the people that you care about and sharing traditions with the children. I feel like I forgot all of that a long time ago, but it's coming back to me now."

"Well, if this is what this experience has brought into your life, then it's been worth it, don't you think?" Bunny asked.

Was it worth it? Maggie wondered. Baking and decorating with the children, making snow angels with John, sewing for Daisy, talking with John under the stars—she nodded and put a hand to her forehead. "Yeah, as crazy as that sounds, yeah."

"Well, I have to tell you," Bunny said in a confidential tone, "that I love the way John is with you around. The kids, too."

Maggie laughed. Her feelings for John were growing stronger each day, and she had wondered how Bunny and Emmett would feel if they knew.

"You've been a nice addition to this family this past week," Bunny went on. "And it makes me happy to see it."

How grateful Maggie was for these accepting, loving people. She turned and hugged Bunny. "Thank you for what you said, Bunny."

"You're so welcome," Bunny whispered.

CHAPTER 32

B rooke returned to work at city hall to finish some preparations for tomorrow's Christmas dance at the community center. She carried the manila envelope of John's papers back to her cubicle.

The visit with John had not gone quite as planned. She had hoped he would be more grateful that she was helping to fast-track his permits. In her imagination, those kids and Maggie had been away somewhere, and John had asked Brooke to stay for dinner. Once she had his undivided attention, she could easily have convinced him how right they were for each other. Instead, she was frustrated.

Why was John so taken with Maggie—a stray he had found on the street, someone he barely knew? Sure, she was pretty, but so was Brooke. What did Maggie have that Brooke didn't? Brooke could see the woman didn't belong here. Why couldn't John see it? He and Brooke had a shared past, a small-town upbringing. They'd gone to high school together and knew the same people.

Noticing the copy of *Aroma Magazine* that had come in her mail, she picked it up.

She felt as she did when something was just at the tip of her tongue, but she couldn't quite remember it. Well, Brooke's memory had often been unreliable, especially when it came to names. But it hardly mattered. Why should she work hard to remember, when she could always ask people their names again? It was kind of humorous, actually. And if it annoyed them, that was their problem, not hers.

She flipped through the magazine until she came to the main feature article, "Making Christmas Unforgettable." And there, above the article, was a picture of Maggie.

She *knew* she had seen her somewhere before! "She's Jennifer Wade."

Now Brooke remembered. She did an internet search for more information and gasped. That was it—she had seen a couple of episodes of Jennifer's show, *Homestyle*, on the Kitchen Network. But what was she doing in Colorado? Did she live here? She scanned the information in Jennifer's bio. No. "From New York," she murmured.

A big-city girl, just as I suspected. Rich and famous, too—definitely *not right for John.*

What should she do? Someone would absolutely want to know that Jennifer was here and had lost her memory.

Scrolling down the page, she found the name of Jennifer's agent. "Paula Marshall." She clicked the

Contact button on the web page, found Paula's phone number, and dialed it on her cell. The phone rang and voice mail picked up.

"Hi, this is Brooke Hanson. I'm calling from North Creek, Colorado. I have some really interesting information regarding your client, Jennifer Wade. If you want to call me back at this number, that would be great. Thank you."

She hung up and gazed thoughtfully at her computer screen. This was good. Maybe the best thing for everyone involved. She wouldn't say anything for now, but in a day or two, Brooke's relationship with John might have a much better chance.

To Brooke's surprise, her cell rang minutes after she left the office. When she answered, the voice on the other end asked, "Hello, is this Brooke Hanson?"

"Yes. Can I help you?"

"This is Paula Marshall, Jennifer Wade's agent. I understand that you know where she is?"

"Yes, she's been staying with the Blake family just outside of North Creek, about an hour outside of Boulder," Brooke said. "They're the ones who found her and took her in."

"Is she all right?"

"Well, she has some kind of memory loss, but yes, actually, she's just fine."

"Has she been terribly, terribly distraught?" Paula asked.

"No, last I saw, she was baking cookies. She seems…happy."

"Happy?" Paula said. "That's good. Let's try to keep it that way. For heaven's sake, we don't want to do anything to upset her. That could lead to… Well, I'm not sure what, but I think we should work on keeping her calm and not upsetting her until we get some medical professionals involved."

Brooke stopped in the street. This was becoming more complicated than she had anticipated. "You don't have to worry. She's been seen by a doctor," Brooke said. "People are caring for her. I just think…" Suddenly, Brooke no longer wanted to keep the secret. She wanted the truth to come out so everything could go back to the way it was before Jennifer Wade showed up. "I just think she should know who she is."

Paula said, "I've known her longer than anyone. I really think I should be the one to deal with this."

"Okay." There was no point arguing.

Paula said, "We're on our way. Thank you for getting in touch."

Brooke hung up. Was she taking the coward's way out? Or was she doing the right thing? Either way, it would all be over soon, and things could go back to normal. Or maybe even better than before.

CHAPTER 33

Maggie sat at the breakfast bar, decorating Christmas sugar cookies with Daisy and Jamie. She piped buttercream frosting from a pastry bag onto the shapes of Christmas trees and stars, and the girls embellished them with colored sugar, jelly beans, red hots, peppermints, gumdrops, and tiny marshmallows. She was having at least as much fun as the girls were. The project felt like baking combined with arts and crafts. A perfect mother-daughter time—Maggie knew Jamie and Daisy weren't her daughters, but she had come to love them almost as if they were, and she was sure they loved her, too. How quickly they had found their way into each other's hearts.

The house smelled of candles and fir trees and vanilla and sugar. The perfect scents. A perfect moment.

"Okay, everybody," John announced from the living room, "everyone gets to open one present today."

"Okay!" Daisy said.

The children didn't need to be told twice. They ran into the living room.

Maggie smiled at their sweet excitement. It was moments like these that made holidays special. Watching them, she had a faint memory of that feeling—an almost magical tingle of anticipation.

The sugar cookies could wait. Basking in the sentimental glow, Maggie joined them in the living room. She sat on the couch near John, and Kyle plopped himself down between them.

"All right," John said. For some reason, he seemed almost as excited as the kids.

"Here. You go first," Jamie said, handing Maggie a present.

"For me?" This was completely unexpected. Why would anyone have bought her a Christmas gift? After all, she'd been here less than a week, and no one knew much about her. *She* knew very little about herself. Could it be something to do with baking or cooking? An apron? Or maybe something practical like hand lotion? Though caught off guard, Maggie was intrigued.

The whole family watched Maggie with eager interest.

"Guess who it's from," Jamie said. Her father took her hand and kissed it.

"Okay." Feeling slightly self-conscious, Maggie opened the box. She gasped when she saw a flash of red and recognized the knitted mittens she and John had come across while window shopping. Beautiful, beautiful mittens, like a pair her mother had made for her long ago. She smiled, picked them up, and hugged them to her with absolute joy.

"How beautiful," Bunny said, joining them. "John, you picked those out?"

"Well, actually, Maggie did, I guess. Right?" John said, his eyes never leaving Maggie's face. He seemed to be pleased with her reaction to the gift. "I mean, you said they gave you a good memory, and I thought we could use all the help that we can get."

"Thank you so much," Maggie said, emotion welling up inside her. "I don't know what to say. They're beautiful. I love them." Holding the mittens close, she wished she had something to give them in return to show them how much the gesture meant to her. "But I didn't get you guys anything." Now that she thought of it, there was a small gift she could give John. She would have to finish it quickly and tuck it behind the tree before they left for the Christmas dance.

"What do you mean?" John asked. "You just being here is like the best Christmas present we could ever ask for. Really, I think we all agree with that, right?"

Bunny nodded.

Kyle and Daisy said, "Yeah!"

Maggie was touched by this. The fact that Bunny and Emmett, the kids, and John were all grateful she was with them buoyed her spirits. Making their family happier was the least she could do for all they had done for her. She stroked Kyle's head.

"Don't you see?" Jamie said. "You brought

Christmas back to our family." She threw her arms around Maggie's neck and put her head on Maggie's shoulder. A moment later, Kyle and Daisy hugged her too, and she wrapped her arms around them all while John smiled. If her memory never came back, at least Maggie knew the connections between her and the kids were real and true. And the connection between her and John, there could be no doubt.

Maggie let herself absorb the warm sincerity in his eyes, the wholehearted acceptance from the kids. For her, the day was already perfect. Feeling more blessed than she could have imagined a week earlier, Maggie closed her eyes and held them. With pure joy.

CHAPTER 34

The air was brisk as John, Maggie, the kids, Emmett, and Bunny went to the community center for the Christmas dance. Dan wasn't with them since he was on business in New Mexico and would be back on Christmas night. Maggie felt pretty wearing Bunny's jade-green dress. John was decked out in a button-down shirt and tie under a black vest, with a black leather jacket—festive, but not formal. He was dashing and handsome in a down-to-earth way that made Maggie feel comfortable around him.

She thought Jamie and Daisy looked adorable with bows in their blonde hair and black bolero jackets over their dresses. Kyle, who really didn't like to dress up, wore a red tee under a navy dress shirt with the sleeves rolled up.

Inside the community center, Maggie glanced around, appreciating the cheerful decor. The community center's Christmas tree was probably fifteen feet tall, decorated with ornaments of gold, silver, and red in a dozen different sizes, red velvet bows, and small white Christmas lights. The stage was decorated with white lights and a green tinsel garland, and throughout the room, star-shaped Mylar balloons floated. The air held the scents of pine, warm apple cider, clove, and cinnamon. An instrumental version of "Deck the Halls" played in the background, and the music made her so happy. To Maggie, everything felt just right.

Bunny and Emmett went to get some punch. The kids called, "Bye, Dad," and headed off to see their friends.

"Okay, bye," John said, his hand lightly touching Maggie's back.

And then Maggie and John were alone, just the two of them. She hardly noticed the other people in the room as she smiled up at him, enjoying the fluttery exhilaration inside her. Here they were, together. Like a date. Like a couple.

"Here, let me get your coat," John said, his hands brushing against her shoulders as he helped her out of the coat and held it for her.

A tingle ran through Maggie. "Thank you." She wanted to say so much more.

Brooke approached them with a smile. "Hi. Merry almost Christmas."

"Merry almost Christmas," John and Maggie replied. Maggie was so giddy with enchantment this evening that not even Brooke could spoil her mood.

"Maggie," Brooke said, "you look just lovely in that dress."

"Oh, thank you. It's Bunny's, actually," Maggie said.

"Oh!"

"And I love that color on you," Maggie told her, referring to Brooke's aubergine dress under a black blazer. "It really brings out your eyes."

Brooke gave a shy smile, as if surprised by the compliment. "Thank you." She opened her mouth as if to say something else, but then seemed to think better of it and merely shook her head.

"We should go find the kids," John told Maggie, resting his hand at the small of her back.

"Okay," Maggie said, feeling the warmth of his hand. *What a wonderful thing to say*, she thought. *We should go find the kids*. It sounded so right. She felt a melting sensation deep inside. She blinked as her eyes got misty. How could she feel so happy and sad at the same time? She finally felt as if she belonged here.

But after Christmas, then what? She had already recalled a few scenes and memories from her past, and any day now, all of it could come crashing back into her mind. Then she would lose this family she had grown to love. She would lose this man she had come to hold so dear.

What do *I feel for him?* It was more than mere affection. Life was so complicated! But not now. Tonight was simple. They were just a man and a woman, together and happy. Her eyes misted over again. This was no time for tears—even happy ones. It was a party. She let John guide her away from Brooke toward the festivities.

"Okay," Brooke repeated, looking after the two of them with concern. "Okay." She sighed.

John and Maggie crossed the room and started mingling. He introduced her to many people she hadn't met yet, including the owners of Open Latte, which was catering the dance. John told Bill and Rita about Maggie's cooking and baking skills, and they had a lively chat. Everybody Maggie met was friendly and welcoming.

Dancing began in earnest as the live band on the stage played upbeat Christmas tunes. Sherrilyn Juarez sang lead on "It's a Merry Christmas." Her grandmother Rita went to refill the refreshment tables. To support their granddaughter by dancing while she sang, Bill swept Maggie out onto the floor and proceeded to demonstrate all of his best swing dance moves for her. John and the children bounced and twirled nearby. Bunny and Emmett demonstrated some sprightly moves, as well.

When the song ended, the audience applauded, and John high-fived each of the kids. Maggie beamed. *What a wonderful father he is.* She couldn't remember much, but even if she could've, she was sure she hadn't felt this happy in years.

A slow song began. Maggie was still smiling at the kids when John approached her. She looked up into his eyes and all of a sudden felt shy. He took her right hand in his left and pulled her gently into his embrace. Her hand rested lightly on his shoulder as they swayed to the music. The warm feeling of his arm around her left her breathless. They moved closer together, so close she could feel the heat of his cheek next to hers. She let her eyes drift shut. A kaleidoscope of butterflies floated in slow, magical swirls inside her. She didn't want to breathe for fear of breaking the spell. She wanted to have time stand still, just like this.

He pulled back slightly to look into her eyes.

"This is nice," Maggie said in a dreamy voice. If this was a dream, she never wanted to wake up.

"Yes, it is," John agreed. "Maggie, I gotta tell you. I know someday you are going back to where you're from. But right here, right now…"

His gaze was intense. What was he trying to say? Was he feeling the same thing she was?

"Yes. Go on," she said, smiling, her voice just above a whisper. But maybe words weren't necessary.

They couldn't know what tomorrow would bring, but for today, they had each other. His arm around her, her hand on his shoulder, and his hand holding hers felt real and solid. Nothing else mattered.

Their heads drifted together. They were just inches apart. Her eyes fluttered closed. *Time, stand still. Please.* The rest of the world faded into the distance until her entire focus consisted only of the two of them together, in this moment of time. They were going to kiss, and there was no rush. She felt his soft breath on her lips.

A voice called out, "Where is she?"

Maggie blinked and looked up, the spell broken.

"Where is she? Uh, oh gosh. I'm sorry. I'm looking for someone."

Across the dance floor, Maggie saw a beautiful woman with long, dark curls, wearing an ivory boiled-wool cardigan over a gray turtleneck. A name sprang to her lips. "Paula!"

John gave Maggie a questioning look.

"Jennifer!" Paula said, weaving through the crowd to Maggie and giving her a kiss on the cheek. "Oh, there you are. Thank goodness. Oh, sweetie, thank goodness. Honey, you had me so worried. We haven't been able to reach you all week. You're a day late returning the rental car, and the agency said they hadn't heard a peep from you. I thought something awful had happened to you." She gestured around at the festivities. "And well, here you are, having fun at a party. Is everything all right?"

"Yeah, everything's fine," she said. But it wasn't. She was disoriented, trying to fit things together in her mind. What was happening?

"Jennifer! Excuse me, excuse me," said a dark, handsome man as he made his way through the crowd toward her. "Hey, I'm so glad you're okay." He leaned in and kissed her cheek.

He looked familiar, but she couldn't quite place him. Why was he kissing her?

The man pointed to John. "Who's this?"

"This is so confusing," Maggie said. She turned and mouthed to John, "I don't know who that is."

Another voice rang out across the hushed crowd. "We found it! We found the car. Recovered everything." Deputy Darren Wilkes hurried into the room.

"*My* car?" Maggie asked.

"You had a car accident. Your vehicle went off the road. We found everything in it. Your bags, ID. Sheriff stayed back to clear up the site. But he sent me with this. You're uh…" The Deputy held up her ID.

But she didn't need to read it. She held up a finger for emphasis. "Jennifer…Wade."

John smiled at her in surprise, apparently realizing she'd remembered this on her own.

Then it hit her full force. "*I'm Jennifer Wade.* I remember my name. And I'm from New York. And this is Paula. My friend. My friend who came looking for me." What a relief it was to know she had people who cared about her! Cared enough to fly across the country to find her. "Thank you," she said to Paula. "And, uh…" she looked in confusion at the man with Paula. She couldn't quite place him yet. A fog still muddled part of her brain.

He gave her a broad, confident smile.

"And this is Brad…" Paula supplied. Her voice trailed off as if she were waiting for Jennifer to finish her sentence.

"Right," Jennifer said, grasping at the explanation. "It's Brad, Paula's boyfriend."

"Uh, no, no," Paula hastened to say, with a chuckle. "Brad, *your* boyfriend."

For a split second, Jennifer tried to process this

information. *Her boyfriend.* That felt wrong, somehow. Jennifer should know whether she had feelings for Brad, just by seeing him again, shouldn't she? John looked stunned. She never wanted to hurt him. How could she care so deeply for John and have no memory of Brad? She couldn't possibly have a boyfriend, no matter what Paula said. "I don't think so," Jennifer said firmly. "So, how did you find me?"

"I had a very helpful phone call from a woman named, uh, Brooke," Paula replied.

"Yeah," Brad confirmed while Paula searched the room with her eyes.

Brooke appeared next to the deputy. "Um, that's me," she confessed.

"So you remembered where you knew me from?" Why would Brooke have withheld such important news?

"It was the interview in *Aroma Magazine*," Brooke said.

"You knew...*when*?" Jennifer asked.

"Last night?" Brooke admitted.

John looked at her in troubled surprise. "And you called them, not us?"

"Why didn't you tell me?" Jennifer asked.

Brooke's face was earnest. "I wanted to tell you as soon as you guys arrived. Everyone just seemed so happy. I'm so sorry."

Jennifer wanted to accuse Brooke of trying to come between Jennifer and John all along. She wanted to yell that it wasn't fair. She wanted to blame Brooke for not sharing the news the moment she read the article in *Aroma Magazine*. But was that really what "Maggie" would have wanted? No. There was no point in holding Brooke responsible. Maggie would not have wanted to miss a single moment of precious time with John and his family.

"It's okay," Jennifer told Brooke. "It's okay that you didn't tell me, because it gave me today." She turned to John. "We had today. We had a lot of days. Thank you so much for everything you've done for me. And thank you, all of you, for making me feel so welcome."

Kyle hugged her. Daisy looked so sad, Jennifer almost started to cry. She put a hand on Kyle's head, wanting to freeze this moment as well. Getting her memory back couldn't tear her apart from people she loved, could it?

"You really should see a doctor in the city," Paula said, taking control, as Jennifer recalled she often did. "So, honey, we gotta go home now."

John looked as if someone had kicked him in the stomach.

Jennifer wanted to put her arms around him and comfort him. But how could she? *She* was the reason he felt awful. She was torn. "But I don't...I don't want to just leave," she said, wiping away a tear. Being in Colorado with him and his family didn't feel strange or new or temporary. It felt right.

"We've got a flight to catch," Paula said. She spread her hands, making a big announcement. "I got you a spot on the network's float for the Christmas Day parade!"

"Next to me," Brad said with a proud grin, as if it were added incentive.

"Yes, right?" Paula said.

Jennifer's heart sank. She had an official commitment on Christmas Day and had no choice but to leave now.

"Don't go," Daisy pleaded, turning to hug Jennifer. Jamie came up next to them and joined in the embrace. John rubbed Jamie's back to comfort her.

Jennifer felt John close beside her. She wished he would hug her like the kids were doing. She needed his comfort and his strength. A part of her very core seemed to be breaking, and she didn't dare look at him yet. It would hurt too much.

She remembered what John had told her about when the children lost their mom and then their dog, Pixie. How he didn't want them to go through the grief of loss again in their young lives. And now she had done that to them. She hated to see them in pain. Her heart had made a promise to all of them, but it seemed her heart had a previous obligation. And she always kept her commitments.

"Oh, sweetheart," Jennifer said, putting her arms around the children. "I...I wish I didn't have to, but I think I do."

"I love you," Daisy said.

"I love you, too," Jennifer told her. "I love all of you." *Including you, John*, she thought. She finally admitted it to herself, but she couldn't say it out loud. She had felt safe and warm with her arms around him. It wasn't just John's house and his kids and his dog that felt like home to her. *John* felt like home. And now it was too late to tell him. She hugged the kids, crying, stroking their hair.

John spoke gently to the children. "Okay, guys. Okay."

Brad averted his eyes, looking distinctly uncomfortable with the emotional scene.

Not ready to let go, Jennifer looked at John. And there it was: sorrow.

"I always knew. I knew you had to go," he said softly. He seemed to be trying to make things easier for her. "Just don't forget us," he added with a wistful smile.

"Never," Jennifer promised.

"We've got to go," Paula prompted. "Excuse us," she said, extricating Jennifer from the children's embrace. "Come, sweetheart."

Jennifer watched the kids huddle against their father for comfort. Why did it have to be this way?

Smiling, Paula took Jennifer by the hand and led her away from John. "Thank you. Thank you so very much." She lowered her voice and spoke in soothing tones to Jennifer. "I have your bags. Everything's going to be there and waiting."

Jennifer's gaze was drawn back to the kids. Kyle's face was pressed to his father's side. Jamie leaned against John for support, and Daisy cried.

Jennifer didn't want to do this—not to the kids, not to herself. Not to John. Her eyes found his and held them. There was so much she wanted to tell him, but she wouldn't have a chance. His own gaze held volumes of unspoken thoughts.

"Bye, kids," Brad said, breaking the connection.

"Thank you," Paula said one last time, taking Jennifer's arm and turning to usher her out. "But we've got to rush."

Jennifer's heart ached so much she could hardly draw a breath. It was all she could do to keep walking. She told herself that she was doing what she was supposed to do. Taking the road of honor. She was a woman who kept her commitments, and she was doing the right thing. But it didn't feel right. She didn't know if she would ever feel right again.

CHAPTER 35

On the way out of North Creek, they stopped at the Blake house for a few minutes to let Jennifer change into more comfortable clothes, which she would send back in a couple of days. She hung the green dress in Daisy and Kyle's closet and caressed the vintage fabric in a kind of goodbye—not just to the dress and how she had felt in it, but to who she had been when she wore it. It was time to go back to reality.

She dressed in jeans, a long-sleeved wine shirt under a coat, and shearling boots. Good layers. Perfect for winter. By contrast, Paula's cowl-necked cashmere sweater, wool coat, and high-heeled boots were far less practical than they were stylish.

On the flight to New York, Jennifer barely spoke. She couldn't let herself think or feel. She had to stay numb. It was the only way she could get through this.

Jennifer felt strangely disoriented as she, Paula, and Brad entered Paula's chic Manhattan apartment.

"Now, I want you," Paula told Jennifer, "to stay a few days here with me. At least until we can get you checked out by a doctor." She set her bag down by the sofa and guided Jennifer to sit before she went on. "Then you can go back to your place."

"I'm…I'm fine, Paula," Jennifer said automatically.

Brad put his coat and bag down. Turning to Jennifer with a bewildered shrug, he asked, "How did you…live out there with those people for a week? I mean it's so…*not* New York." He chuckled at his joke and paused to let her answer. When Jennifer didn't respond, he concluded, "Okay. Um…I need a drink."

Ever the gracious hostess, Paula said, "Okay. You know where it is. Make yourself at home." She sat on the sofa beside Jennifer. "Darling, how are you feeling? Are you happy to be back?"

"I don't know," Jennifer said. How did she feel? Nothing felt quite *right* at the moment.

So not New York, Brad had said. Jennifer used to enjoy the frenetic pace of life in the Big Apple. New York was home, but she no longer felt at home. Her apartment was here. Her job was here. Her friend Meredith was here. Paula was here. But her heart was still in the mountains of Colorado. She winced. How ironic that while her memory was lost, she had worried that no one loved her enough to come searching for her. She'd longed for her memories. And now that she had them, some of the dearest memories were those she had made with John and the children.

With her usual optimism, Paula said, "Well, you will feel better once you get back into the routine of things. Lots of exciting things happened while you were away. We got a call from, uh... You know what? Maybe we'll talk about this a little later." Paula got up and took off her coat. "I'll go put the kettle on."

John's house felt too quiet. And empty. All day long, he'd walked around the house expecting to see Maggie at any moment, only to remember...

He had been through the pain of loss when Julie died. Here it was again. Different, but still agonizing. The kids were hurting. John tried to act normal for their sake. But he was hurting, too. He kept telling himself he'd known all along Maggie would have to leave. Why had he let himself care for her so much? Had it been worth the risk?

It had only been twenty-four hours since the Christmas dance. Last night, he'd held Maggie in his arms, ready to accept that some higher purpose had brought her to him. Their angels had touched.

And then, the thing he had been dreading had happened: her memories returned, her friends came for her, and his time with her ended.

At the end, the kids had clung to John and were inconsolable. His eyes had filled with tears. For a short while, he had dared to let himself dream, but then, all the hopes he had allowed himself to feel had faded to a burning ache as he'd watched Maggie—no, *Jennifer*—leave.

Now, only a day later, John made his rounds, tucking the kids into bed. When he got to Daisy and

Kyle's room, the light was on, and Daisy was propped up on one arm in her canopied bed, writing. She wore a red thermal shirt and colorful fleece pajama pants.

He sat down on the multicolored bedspread. He didn't really have the heart to scold her for being up past her bedtime. Today had been sad and subdued enough in their house. "What are you doing awake? You should be asleep, young lady," he said gently.

She sat up, pulled her knees to her chest, and wrapped her arms around them. "I'm writing a letter to Santa asking him for what I want," Daisy confided.

"Oh. Well, that's a very smart thing to do. What do you want?" *It must be fairly important if she stayed up to write a letter.*

"It's a secret, or else it won't come true." Daisy barely paused for a moment before saying, "But I can tell you. I want him to bring Maggie back on his sleigh."

John wished it were so simple. If only his daughter's innocent wish could be granted. But Jennifer had her old life back now, and they had no rightful claim to her.

John picked up the paper and pencil. "Oh. Well, I will make sure Santa gets your letter. And you get to sleep, okay?" She lay down, and he pulled the blanket up over her. "Come on now, get in there. Sweet dreams." He kissed her and turned out the lamp.

Holding Daisy's letter, he went to the living room and sat by the fire. Why had he let himself fall for Maggie? He had known the risk. But wasn't that part of life? Love meant opening yourself up to the risk of pain. He never once questioned whether Julie had been worth the pain he'd suffered once she was gone.

Gazing into the fire, he realized he'd been shielding himself from love since Julie died. To prove his love for Julie, he had believed he had to hold on to every memory, preserving each one. He had dedicated himself completely to their children, frozen in mourning, and giving up any other hope for love.

But Julie had never asked him for that. In those last few weeks before she passed away, she told him, "Make our home a happy place—for you and for the kids. If that means falling in love again, you have my blessing. Don't forget"—she winked—"this is where the magic happens."

While Maggie was with them, the house *was* happy. John had been the one who wasn't ready to let go, fearing he would forget, fearing that if he let go of any memory, he would lose what he and Julie had shared. Had he finally let go only to find he'd missed his chance?

CHAPTER 36

Jennifer sat in Paula's living room, holding the red mittens she had gotten for Christmas. Brad was on the other side of the sofa, reading email on his cell phone.

"I am just going to pop over to your apartment and pick up a few things since everything was destroyed in the crash," Paula said. Apparently, even though Jennifer's bags had been recovered from the crashed rental car, most of the clothing had been ruined. Jennifer found she didn't care about the clothes at all.

She noticed the painting behind Paula. Now the *painting* was something she cared about. "Paula, how long have you had that?"

Paula turned to look at the artwork. "What, the painting? Just a few years."

Jennifer stared at it. "It's beautiful. I know the artist." She missed Dan and his no-nonsense view of the world. She missed so much...

"Honey, why don't you go and soak in the tub,"

Paula suggested. "I will be back before you know it. Brad?"

Brad looked up from his cell phone. "Hmm?"

"You're going to drive me."

He looked at his cell again. "Yeah, sure, just let me know when you're ready."

Jennifer stroked the red mittens, lost in thoughts of the past week.

"I'm just going to grab my purse," Paula said.

Brad glanced up briefly and noticed Jennifer holding the red mittens. "Whatcha got there? Hand-me-downs?"

Jennifer froze. Her eyes went wide, and she wondered if Brad had any idea he'd just insulted her. Earlier, he'd implied that being in North Creek must have been difficult to endure, and now he had stepped on the precious memories her mittens evoked—of her mother and of John. It was almost a relief to understand that she and Brad were so fundamentally different. Brad's affection for her had a goal. He was most interested in Jennifer for the boost their careers would get if they were together. Just as Ashton had only cared about her as a status symbol of the perfect life he pretended to have.

Perfect. That's the problem.

For the longest time, Jennifer had believed she needed to be perfect to be loved—the perfect wife, the perfect image, the perfect TV host. Jennifer had wanted her viewers to have the perfect experience. That idea hadn't come from her mother, though.

Ashton had used her as a prop for success in his high-society business and social world. He'd undermined her self-confidence, pointing out every flaw. She'd yielded to the power he'd held over her...hoping to get a family in exchange. But unlike Brad and Ashton, John didn't want to use her as a showpiece or ride her coattails. John accepted her without trying to control her. His family freely offered her encouragement, admiration, appreciation, and love. And John believed Jennifer's presence enriched him and his family. Brad, on the other hand, like Ashton, focused on outward appearance.

"Brad, who do you think that I am?" she asked, gazing at her mittens.

He answered without hesitation, as if it were self-explanatory. "You know who you are. You're Jennifer Wade."

Jennifer looked him in the eye then. "I think that the definition of who that is has changed," she said. "Or maybe I'm actually now who I was always meant to be." Jennifer decided there was no point in trying to clarify it further. She didn't want to hurt him. He didn't deserve that. He had flown halfway across the country to bring her back. "I'm really sorry, Brad. You're a wonderful guy," she began.

He winced at her words and nodded, as if he understood what was coming.

She rushed on. "And you're going to make some lucky woman incredibly happy. It's just not going to be me." She stood up, holding her coat and red mittens, and started toward the door. She knew now exactly who she was and where she was supposed to be.

Paula returned to the room with her purse. Jennifer stopped her. "Paula, you don't need to go to my apartment. I..." Jennifer searched for the words to explain what she was feeling, but she didn't need them. Her friend understood instantly.

"Wow. Stop. Make no apology." Smiling, Paula took Jennifer's hands in hers. "Do not explain. You go do what you gotta do. I'll make sure that there's a ticket waiting for you."

Jennifer hugged her. Somehow, her dear friend comprehended in an instant what it had taken Jennifer too long to recognize. "Thank you, Paula. You're an angel. And a wonderful friend." She looked at Brad and then at Paula again. "I wish you both a very wonderful Christmas."

"Oh, sweetie, merry Christmas to you, too," Paula said.

As Jennifer left, she heard Brad ask Paula, "Okay, so am I driving you or not?"

In the cab on the way to the airport, Jennifer made a phone call.

Paula answered on the first ring. "Jennifer?"

"I have a question," Jennifer said. "Does my contract state that my show has to be made in Manhattan? I mean, could we shoot it anywhere?"

"Darlin', I've known you weren't always happy living in New York, and when we found you at that party in Colorado, you looked happier than I've ever seen you. There's nothing about New York in your contract." Paula chuckled. "Now, you just let me know when you decide what you want to do, and leave the rest to me. I know just how to pitch it to the network, if you want to shoot the show somewhere else."

Hanging up the phone with a happy sigh, Jennifer leaned back in the taxi, took out her red mittens, and hugged them to her heart.

CHAPTER 37

It snowed on Christmas morning in North Creek. John gazed out his bedroom window at a winter wonderland. Four inches of fresh snow had fallen since he'd shoveled the driveway on Christmas Eve. No need to shovel again. Other than family, there would be no deliveries or visitors.

He put on a pair of jeans and a burgundy Henley shirt. Maggie—no, Jennifer—had said the color looked good on him. He went down to the kitchen, made coffee, and stood alone drinking it. His morning coffee ritual felt incomplete now. As he looked at the beautifully decorated Christmas tree, he was struck by the sheer force of how much he missed her. For a few minutes, he allowed the loneliness to envelop him. But then he pushed it aside. He had to, for the kids and for himself. He had to accept that what he and Jennifer had shared was past. A beautiful memory. He was an optimist, and he would focus on the good in his life. It was a beautiful white Christmas, and John was determined to make it merry.

Bunny and Emmett arrived, and the kids rushed downstairs, wearing their pajamas. They all gathered around the tree in the living room to open presents.

It was the most beautiful Christmas in years. And John felt more loss than he had felt in years. He couldn't be sorry Jennifer had come into their lives. They were all richer for it. Ornaments chosen with love. Homemade decorations hung with care. Traditions renewed. Still, there was a Jennifer-shaped hole in their family. The kids felt it. Bunny knew. Ever since the Christmas dance, Bunny had spoken to him in that especially gentle tone she had used after Julie died.

As she had for the past three years, Bunny passed out the packages. She started with the special gifts from John.

"Here you go, Jamie," Bunny said, handing her a gift.

Jamie opened hers and gave a squeal of delight when she saw the microscope. "I love it. Daddy, will you show me what you look at when you put a sample on a slide?"

"That's a great idea," John said. "Plus, there's a whole book of experiments we can do."

"Kyle, here you go," Bunny said, passing his present to him.

Kyle tore the paper open. "Whoa—a telescope? That's the best! Thanks, Dad."

"You know I love to look at the stars. I thought

maybe we could spend some time stargazing together," John said.

Bunny gave Daisy a box. "I bet you can't guess what that is."

Daisy rattled it. "A puzzle? Building blocks?" She ripped the wrapping away to reveal the toolbox. She looked surprised, but not disappointed.

John pointed at the colorful picture on the outside of the box. "That's a real hammer and screwdriver and measuring tape and tools like I have in my own toolbox. And you know what we're going to use them for?" John asked. "Remember when you guys helped me build that squirrel picnic table? Well, you and I are going to build a house for Sally."

Daisy bounced up and down with glee. "Sally's house! Yay!"

John couldn't have asked for a better reaction from the kids. What a wonderful tradition Julie had started. The thought was comforting now, not painful.

"John..." Bunny fetched a gift from behind the tree and gave it to him.

The package was wrapped in folds of clear cellophane, tied at the top with white ribbons—not the kind of wrapping Bunny or the kids would have used. It was hard to see what was inside.

"What is this?" John asked.

Bunny gave him a secretive smile. "I think you're going to like it. Open it."

He checked the tag automatically and felt a small burst of happiness at what he saw. "Hey, guys," John told the kids, "it's from Jennifer." He opened the cellophane to reveal the most wonderful gingerbread house he had ever seen. It was shaped like a barn, and on a sign above the door, the words "Animal Hospital" were written in white icing. Marzipan animals and people stood by the barn. Sugary snow and icicles clung to the gingerbread roof. John could hardly believe it. Touched, he recalled what she'd said about honoring Julie by converting the barn into an animal hospital. A clinic in their barn wouldn't be impersonal like an office in some professional building downtown. It would be a tribute.

"Wow," Daisy said at the same time as Kyle said, "Cool."

Jamie said, "It's beautiful."

All three kids crowded around their father to get a better look.

"The coolest present ever." Daisy said.

"From Maggie?" Kyle asked.

"Look at all the animals. I wish I could take a bite," Daisy said.

Jamie studied the details. "It's our barn with the animals. And there's you, Dad."

Kyle leaned across his sister to get a better look. "It's all of us," he said.

"It's the prettiest thing I've ever seen," Bunny said. She put a hand on John's arm and gave him an understanding look.

"It's amazing," John agreed. The love and effort Jennifer had put into it were clear in every detail. He needed her. His family loved her. Before she'd gotten her memories back, he'd tried to resist falling for her. Worried that she had a family, he hadn't wanted to cause them pain.

John had been up most of the night, reading everything he could find about Jennifer Wade on the internet. She had no children, no current husband or fiancé. And her boyfriend—she had barely recognized the man and had certainly not remembered their relationship. Her surprise at finding out about Brad had been genuine. The sportscaster had a playboy image and a history of dating supermodels. John couldn't judge him based on that information alone, though. If Jennifer loved Brad, John could accept it. But if she didn't, then…

Then what? She deserved a choice about her future life—that was what. He loved her. Did she feel the same way? Suddenly, he made a decision.

"That's it, guys," he said, looking around at his family. "Enough of this. Everybody up. I want you to get your coats on. Because we are going to get her." Nobody asked who he meant by "her." He carefully set the gingerbread building down. "Come on! Coats on, boots on. Coats and boots. You got it?"

A weight lifted from John's heart. It felt light, as if it were dancing inside him. John didn't want to waste time packing. They would figure this trip out as they went.

Everyone from Emmett to Daisy scrambled to get

their cold-weather gear on with laughter and happy conversation.

"Where's my boots?" John asked. Urgency built inside him as he rummaged around on the floor. The few seconds it took to find them seemed far too long. They were going to see Jennifer! Standing up, he hopped on one foot and then the other while he put his boots on.

When they were finally all ready, he opened the door.

And there stood Jennifer. Parked behind her in the snow was a powerful sport utility vehicle.

"Maggie!" Kyle said.

Stunned, John just stared for a few seconds, unable to believe it was true.

Daisy bolted through the doorway and hugged her. "Maggie, you came back."

A moment later, Kyle and Jamie were in her arms, too. "You came back!" Jamie said.

John's heart gave a leap at the beautiful sight. *She's really here.* His snow angel. He stepped outside, and she looked up at him, radiating happiness.

"I can't believe it. Christmas!" Kyle said. "Best Christmas ever."

"Merry Christmas," Jennifer said, kissing Jamie's head.

John noticed that Jennifer was wearing the mittens he had bought her.

"Merry Christmas," Jamie said, hugging her.

"Kids, come in," Bunny said in a soft voice, collecting Jamie, Daisy, and Kyle. "Let's give them some

privacy. Come on, let's go open some more presents."
She and the children went inside and closed the door,
leaving Jennifer and John alone on the doorstep.

Bless Bunny, John thought.

He was overwhelmed with joy—for his kids, for
himself, for Jennifer. He didn't know if his heart could
hold any more happiness without bursting.

Alone with John, Jennifer suddenly felt unsure of
herself.

"Hi," he said.

"Hi." She couldn't look away from his intense blue
gaze. She didn't want to. She found herself tongue-tied.
She had been rehearsing a speech in her mind all the
way here, but now her words tangled and tripped over
each other. She hesitated as doubt took hold of her.
Until now, she had assumed John felt as she did, but
what if she was wrong? He had only known *Maggie*,
not Jennifer. And it was Maggie who had fallen in love
with John, yet she had never told him.

Jennifer had finally found what she'd been looking
for, for as long as she could remember. She couldn't
bear it if she lost that now. But what could she do,
other than make her case, and then wait to see how
John truly felt? Finally, she forced herself to speak.

"I'm Jennifer Wade. From New York. I don't have
any family. I'm not sure if I'll ever get one hundred
percent of my memory back."

John smiled at the mention of memories.

Hoping it was a good sign, Jennifer forged ahead. "But I know that I love your kids. And I love your dog. And I'm a pretty decent cook." There was so much more to tell him. What did he need to know right now to make a decision? She racked her brain. He'd probably want to know that she was crazy about him—about his kindness and compassion, about what a great father and friend he was. She drew a deep breath.

Before she could go on, John said in a soft voice, "I like Jennifer from New York as much as Maggie from North Creek—right, you know that?"

"You do?" Her pulse raced.

"Yeah."

Was that enough? He liked her. But did he love her? Could they make something out of what they had together? Jennifer swallowed. "Well, what would you say to Jennifer from North Creek?"

His eyes shut briefly, as if he were savoring a delicious moment. His voice was soft as he replied, "I would say I like that a lot." He opened his eyes and held her gaze as he slowly closed the distance between them.

As if drawn by a magnet, Jennifer swayed ever so slightly toward him. The world seemed to go still, as if holding its breath. Their lips touched, and his warm mouth pressed against hers in a sweet, tender kiss that held the promise of many more to come.

"Merry Christmas," he said.

She felt as if a million tiny lights began twinkling

inside her, giving her a happy feeling from head to toe. "Merry Christmas."

Jennifer and John held each other for a long, long time before either of them spoke again.

"Did I interrupt something?" she said at last. "It looked like you were going somewhere when I arrived."

He gave a soft laugh. "We didn't have *plans* so much as we had a goal: we wanted to convince you to come back here with us, no matter what. It was like we all realized at the same time that you were missing from our family and we needed you."

"That's kind of how I felt, too." Indescribable warmth spread through her. She touched one of her mittened hands to the center of his chest, mittens like the ones her mother had so lovingly knitted long ago. Her throat tightened. "A whole tidal wave of memories came rushing back. And when they were all done washing over me, I was left with this rock-solid belief inside me that *this* is where I belonged."

John stroked her cheek with the backs of his fingers. She leaned in to the caress, and he cupped his hand to her cheek. His bare fingers on her face sent a tingle through her.

He kissed her again, longer this time.

"So, how do you want this to work?" he asked.

She rested her head against his shoulder and leaned into his warmth.

"Are you sure you want to move here?" he asked. "What about your job? Are you going to quit?"

Jennifer froze. "Is...is that what you want?"

He took her face in his hands and tilted it so he could look into her eyes. "I would never ask you to give that up. That's your decision. I'll share you with the whole world, if that's what you want."

Jennifer got lost for a moment in the depth of his eyes, and she knew it was true: he would never force her to do anything she didn't want to. She relaxed. "In that case, I have some ideas about how to work things out."

EPILOGUE

The next December, in the kitchen on the new set of her TV show, Jennifer held a roasted turkey on a platter and marveled at how her life had changed this year. The kitchen set was built under the eight-pillared bandstand in North Creek's town center. Several inches of snow covered the roof and the ground around the open-air set. Jennifer wore a red Christmas top with a long fleece jacket. On the counters all around her lay the evidence of her Christmas cooking exuberance: rice, macaroni and cheese, brussels sprouts, green beans, a medley of steamed broccoli and carrots and cauliflower, and tins of cellophane-wrapped cookies.

Setting down the platter of turkey garnished with radishes, flat-leaf parsley, and yellow cherry tomatoes, Jennifer absolutely beamed with happiness. It was a real turkey this year, not a "perfect" prop turkey with makeup on it.

"Well, I hope you've all really enjoyed our holiday edition of *Homestyle*," she said. She motioned for John,

Jamie, Kyle, and Daisy to join her on camera, and they all rushed into the TV kitchen.

"I'm Jennifer Blake." She never got tired of saying her new name. John had proposed to her on Valentine's Day, Paula had thrown a bachelorette party with all of Jennifer's best friends, and most of North Creek had attended John and Jennifer's wedding in the community center. The staff of *Homestyle* had gone above and beyond to help Jennifer with sewing, decorating, and floral arrangements. Now Jennifer held up her left hand to show the diamond ring and wedding band she wore, but there was something far more valuable that she wanted to share with her viewers. She glowed with joy, spreading out her arms to hug John and the kids. "And this is my family."

John carved off a piece of turkey and gave it to Kyle, who tasted it.

"How is it?" Jennifer asked.

"Good!" Kyle exclaimed.

They all laughed.

Jennifer reflected on all that had happened since her last Christmas show. The past year had been a whirlwind of wonderful events. Jennifer had moved to North Creek. Production on her show had relocated to Colorado a few months later. Then came the wedding. After a short honeymoon, John and Jennifer had taken the kids on a family vacation to Disney World. They'd spent months renovating the barn. And just a couple of months ago, John had surprised the family with a puppy and a kitten. Their household overflowed with love and laughter.

"And from all of our family and everyone here at North Creek, we wish you a very merry Christmas," Jennifer said, waving to her audience.

"Merry Christmas!" her family chorused.

"And that's a cut," said her director, Ian, from in front of the set.

"That seemed to go pretty good," John said, radiating pride in Jennifer.

"Yeah." Jennifer beamed down at Jamie, Kyle, and Daisy, and then smiled up at him. "All I know is this is a Christmas I'll never forget."

Around them, the crew began packing up cameras, cables, and microphones.

John pulled Jennifer closer. They kissed, oblivious to the commotion around them. Afterward, they leaned their heads together, hugging the kids and enjoying the moment.

"Hey, now that this is wrapped up, why don't we start planning our party for the Julie Blake Memorial Animal Hospital?" John said. They had hired a general contractor to convert the barn into a two-story animal hospital based on plans that John and Jennifer had drawn up. Even the kids had participated in parts of the renovation, each using their own toolkit. The renovated barn had a serene mountain feel to it, with wood and fieldstone in every room and a rocky waterfall in the reception area. Stenciled phrases on the walls expressed the hospital's mission statements.

John's favorite was, "Where the magic happens." He tousled Kyle's hair. "What should we do at the party?"

Jennifer gazed lovingly at John and the kids. "Anything that makes good memories."

RECIPE: HOLIDAY ROAST BEEF WITH ROOT VEGETABLES

A Hallmark Original Recipe

In *A Christmas to Remember*, Jennifer (otherwise known as Maggie) brings an amazing platter to the table. "It's a holiday roast with root vegetables," she says. "You are a really, really, good cook," John says, as the family looks on in awe of her culinary talents. Impress everyone with this delicious rosemary roast beef surrounded with olive oil and herb-roasted potatoes and root vegetables…and make some unforgettable memories.

Yield: 6 servings
Prep Time: 30 minutes
Cook Time: 90 minutes
Total Time: 2 hours

INGREDIENTS

Rosemary Roast Beef:
- ¼ cup olive oil, divided
- 1 (3 to 4 pound) boneless ribeye roast
- 1 tablespoon chopped garlic
- 1 tablespoon fresh rosemary, chopped
- 1 tablespoon kosher salt
- ½ tablespoon freshly ground black pepper

Roasted Root Vegetables:
- 1 bag (1½ pounds) fingerling potatoes, halved
- 1 pound rainbow carrots, peeled
- 2 golden (or red) beets, skin-on, trimmed
- ½ red onion, peeled, cut into wedges
- 3 tablespoons olive oil
- kosher salt and freshly ground black pepper to taste
- 1 tablespoon fresh thyme, chopped
- fresh rosemary sprigs (optional)

DIRECTIONS

1. To prepare roast beef: place a large heavy

ovenproof skillet (such as cast iron) in oven and preheat the oven to 500 degrees F.

2. When oven is heated, remove hot skillet and place on stovetop over high heat. Add 2 tablespoons olive oil to skillet and heat until oil is shimmering; add roast and sear on all sides to brown (about 5 minutes). Remove skillet from heat.

3. Reduce oven heat to 350 degrees F.

4. Combine 2 tablespoons olive oil, garlic, rosemary, salt and black pepper in small bowl and mix to blend; spread evenly over top of browned roast.

5. Transfer skillet to 350 degrees F. oven and roast uncovered for 75 to 90 minutes, or until meat thermometer reads 135 degrees F. (medium-rare) or to desired doneness. Remove from oven. Cover loosely with foil and let rest 15 minutes before slicing.

6. To prepare roasted root vegetables: toss vegetables in olive oil to coat, season with salt, black pepper and thyme. Arrange oiled vegetables on a baking sheet.

7. Roast root vegetables uncovered for 60 minutes or until tender when pierced with a fork and potatoes are golden, turning occasionally. Remove from oven. Let beets

cool slightly; using a paring knife, remove skins and slice each beet in quarters.

8. To serve: Slice roast beef and arrange on a large platter. Surround roast beef with roasted vegetables. Garnish platter with rosemary sprigs, if desired.

Thanks so much for reading *A Christmas to Remember*. We hope you enjoyed it!

You might like these other books from Hallmark Publishing:

Journey Back to Christmas
Christmas in Homestead
Love You Like Christmas
A Heavenly Christmas
A Dash of Love
Love Locks
The Perfect Catch
Like Cats and Dogs
Dater's Handbook

For information about our new releases and exclusive offers, sign up for our free newsletter at hallmarkchannel.com/hallmark-publishing-newsletter

You can also connect with us here:

Facebook.com/HallmarkPublishing

Twitter.com/HallmarkPublish

CPSIA information can be obtained
at www.ICGtesting.com
Printed in the USA
LVHW03s1353080918
589432LV00001B/1/P